"I have yet to tell you my proposition,"
Angelo murmured, and tilted her face to his
when she would have looked away.

"I will set you up with your first big job. You won't need to invest in any equipment. I'll even throw in a small car. You can pay me back when you start making money or if the cottage is sold." He shrugged. "Or you can not pay me back at all. It's immaterial...."

Rosie blinked. Never had such soothingly spoken words carried such dangerous intent. She was listening to him propose a pact with the Devil. Her mouth parted and she made an inarticulate, strangled sound under her breath.

"I know. Thrilling, isn't it? And just when you thought your ship had sunk."

"I can't believe I'm hearing this. I'm not a...a..."

"I think I know the word you're striving to say, but let's leave that unspoken. I like to think that what we have here is the perfect arrangement."

Dear Reader,

We have exciting news! As I'm sure you've noticed, the Harlequin Presents books you know and love have a brand-new look, starting this month. They look *sensational!* Don't you agree?

But don't worry—nothing else about the Presents books has changed. You'll still find eight unforgettable love stories every month, with alpha heroes, empowered heroines and stunning international destinations all topped with passion and a sensual attraction that burns as brightly as ever.

Don't miss any of this month's exciting reads:

Lynne Graham's *The Billionaire's Trophy*
Kate Hewitt's *An Inheritance of Shame*
Lucy Monroe's *Prince of Secrets*
Caitlin Crews, *A Royal Without Rules*
Annie West, *Imprisoned by a Vow*
Cathy Williams, *A Deal with Di Capua*
Michelle Conder, *Duty at What Cost?*
Michelle Smart, *The Rings That Bind*

I hope you're as pleased with our new look as we are. Drop by www.Harlequin.com to let us know what you think.

Joanne Grant
Senior Editor
Harlequin Presents

Cathy Williams

A DEAL WITH DI CAPUA

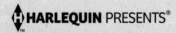
HARLEQUIN PRESENTS®

Recycling programs
for this product may
not exist in your area.

ISBN-13: 978-0-373-13172-3

A DEAL WITH DI CAPUA

Copyright © 2013 by Cathy Williams

HARLEQUIN®
™ www.Harlequin.com

Printed in U.S.A.

CATHY WILLIAMS was born in the West Indies and has been writing Harlequin® romances for some fifteen years. She is a great believer in the power of perseverance as she had never written anything before (apart from school essays a lifetime ago!), and from the starting point of zero has now fulfilled her ambition to pursue this most enjoyable of careers. She would encourage any would-be writer to have faith and go for it! She lives in the beautiful Warwickshire countryside with her husband and three children, Charlotte, Olivia and Emma. When not writing, she is hard-pressed to find a moment's free time in between the millions of household chores, not to mention being a one-woman taxi service for her daughters' never-ending social lives. She derives inspiration from the hot, lazy, tropical island of Trinidad (where she was born), from the peaceful countryside of middle England and, of course, from her many friends, who are a rich source of plots and are particularly talkative when it comes to describing Harlequin Presents heroes. It would seem, from their complaints, that tall, dark and charismatic men are way too few and far between! Her hope is to continue writing romance fiction and providing those eternal tales of love for which, she feels, we all strive.

Other titles by Cathy Williams available in ebook:

CHAPTER ONE

ROSIE HAD NEVER been to a cremation before. Even when her dad had died eight years before, there had been a funeral. Friends—and he had had a surprising number of them, bearing in mind he had spent the majority of his life blearily watching the sun rise and set from the bottom of a whisky glass—had come to pay their respects. Rosie had known few of them. Her own friends had tagged along to give her moral support. At the age of eighteen, she had needed it. From recollection, a distant cousin who had turned out to live a scant three blocks away, in an impoverished two-bedroomed bungalow on a council estate remarkably similar to theirs, had shown up and expressed regret that he hadn't been a more consistent family member.

For all his drunken ways and love of the bottle her father had been a jovial alcoholic and the number of people who had turned out on that brilliantly hot summer day had been testimony to that.

But this…

She had arrived late. It was bitterly cold and a series of small mishaps had made the journey far longer and more arduous than it should have been: Ice on the tracks. Rush hour on the tube. Signal problems as she had neared Earl's Court. It hadn't helped that she had purposefully decided to arrive late so that she could sneak into the back of the chapel and disappear before the service was finished. She had anticipated blending into the crowds.

Hovering now at the back, Rosie felt her heart begin to thud at the scant clutch of people who had shown up for the cremation of Amanda Di Capua, née Amanda Wheeler. Having made the effort to attend the ceremony, she was now desperate to leave, but her unsteady legs had a will of their own. They propelled her forwards so that she neared the group at the front. She kept her eyes firmly fixed on the plump middle-aged man addressing them in a crisp, no-nonsense voice.

Of course, *he* would be there: Angelo Di Capua. Why kid herself that she hadn't seen him? The instant she had stepped into the chapel her eyes had swivelled in his direction. He was easy to spot, but then hadn't he always been? Three years was not nearly long enough for her to have buried the memory of just how tall, how striking, how impossibly good-looking he was. In a packed room, he had always had the ability to stand out. It was just the way he was built.

The horrible, sickening nervous tension that had begun to build over a week ago when she had received that phone call informing her of Amanda's death—when she had decided that she would attend the funeral because Mandy had, after all, once been her closest friend—was spiralling into an unstoppable wave of nausea.

She forced herself to breathe and drew her thick coat tighter around her.

She wished that she had brought Jack along with her but he had wanted no part of it. His bitterness towards their one-time friend ran even deeper than hers.

The service ended whilst she was still lost in her thoughts and she felt the blood drain away from her face as the group of mismatched people began to turn around. She found that she couldn't really recall any of the ceremony at all. The coffin had disappeared behind a curtain. In a few minutes, another batch of mourners would be arriving to replace them.

Angelo would surely come over to speak to her. Even *he* had some rudimentary politeness, and she forced herself to smile and walk forwards as though she was happy to mingle with the handful of people nearing her.

Angelo was among them. Beautiful, sexy Angelo. How must he be taking the death of his young wife? And had he even seen Rosie yet? She wondered whether there was still time to flee the scene but it was too late: a young woman was walking towards her, holding out her hand and introducing herself as Lizzy Valance.

"I phoned you. Remember?" She wiped her eyes with a handkerchief, which she stuffed into the top of the black dress that barely seemed equipped for the job of restricting some of the biggest breasts Rosie had ever seen in her life.

"Yes. Of course…"

"I got your name from Mandy's address book. Plus you were logged in her mobile phone, but I would have got hold of you anyway, cos she always talked about you."

"Oh really?" Rosie's mouth twisted. Out of the corner of her eye, she could see Angelo talking to the vicar while glancing surreptitiously at his watch. He hardly looked like a grieving husband, but then what did she know? She had seen neither him nor Amanda for a very long time, had no idea how life had treated them. She was dimly aware of Lizzy talking, reminiscing over the good times she and Mandy had had, although it seemed those times had become fewer and further between towards the end because of Mandy's drinking.

Rosie didn't want to know. She didn't want to hear about

her ex-friend's trials and tribulations. The times of feeling sympathy for Amanda were long over.

"How did she die?" She interrupted Lizzy abruptly. "You just mentioned an accident—was anyone else involved?" Whatever conversation Angelo had been having with the vicar was at an end and he was turning around towards her. Rosie focused on the small, curvy brunette with the massive bosoms and willed herself into a state of composure but she had to clasp her hands tightly together in front of her to stop them from shaking.

"Thankfully, no. But she had been drinking. It's awful. I told her over and over again that she should get some help, but she never wanted to admit that she had a problem, and she was such fun when…you know…"

"Excuse me. I really have to go."

"But we're all going back to the little pub by her house."

"I'm sorry." Rosie could sense Angelo walking towards her, breaking free of the twenty or so people around him. The urge to run away as fast as her feet could take her was so overpowering that she thought she might faint.

She shouldn't have come. Life was a tough business and there was no room for nostalgia. She, Jack and Amanda might have started their story together, but it certainly hadn't ended up that way, and she just should have let sleeping dogs lie.

She had known that she would see Angelo here. How could she have kidded herself that she wouldn't have been affected? She had given her heart to him, lock, stock and barrel, and he had taken it, broken it and walked off into the sunset with her best friend. Had she really imagined that she had managed to put all that behind her sufficiently to face him once again?

Lizzy had drifted away, leaving her standing on her own, a prime target for the man bearing down on her.

"Rosie Tom. Well, well, well, you're the last person I expected to see here. No, maybe I should rephrase that—you're the last person welcome here."

Of course he had seen her. The second the brief service had concluded and he had half-turned, he had spotted Rosie and instantly he'd felt every muscle in his body, every pore and nerve-ending, spasm painfully with the combined weight of loathing and a certain heightened awareness that angered him almost as much as the sight of her did.

In the winter-infused chapel, she was radiantly striking. Tall and slender as a reed, with that peculiar shade of vibrant auburn hair that never failed to draw attention. She was pale and looked as though, with that hair colouring, she should have had freckles, but her skin was satin-smooth, creamy and unblemished and her eyes were the colour of sherry.

She had the glorious, other-worldly beauty of a woman designed to make men lose their minds. Angelo's mouth thinned with displeasure as he fought to stop the floodgates to the past that were opening up.

"This is a public place," Rosie said coolly. "You might not welcome me here, but I have every right to pay my respects."

"Don't make me laugh. You and Amanda parted as sworn enemies. How did you hear about her death anyway?"

She had had her hair cut. The last time he had seen her, it had been long, tumbling over her shoulders and down her back. Now it was still wavy, but cut in a graduating bob that fell to her shoulders. She looked as chic and eye-catching as she always had.

"I had a call from Lizzy, her friend."

"And you immediately thought that you would bury

the hatchet and rush here to shed big crocodile tears. Do me a favour."

Rosie took a deep breath. She found that she couldn't quite look at him. Too many memories. Not that it mattered whether she actually looked at him or not. In her mind, his image was stamped with ruthless efficiency. The raven-black hair close-cropped; those fabulous eyes that were a peculiar shade of opaque green; the harsh, unforgiving angles of his face that heightened his sexual appeal rather than diminished it; a body that was lean and muscular and lightly bronzed.

"I wasn't going to shed any tears," she said quietly. "But we grew up together. And, now that I've come, I think it's time for me to leave. I just… Whatever's happened, Angelo, I'm sorry for your loss."

Angelo threw back his head and laughed. "You're sorry for my loss? We'd better step outside, Rosie, because if we don't I might just burst out laughing again, and somehow that doesn't seem appropriate for the inside of a chapel."

Before she could protest, her arm was in a vice-like grip and she was being frog-marched out, her breath coming and going in staccato bursts, her brain in complete shutdown mode.

"You're hurting me!"

"Really? Surprisingly, I don't honestly care." They were outside, standing to one side in the bitterly cold, gathering gloom. "Now, why the hell have you shown up here?"

"I told you. I know there's a lot of water under the bridge, but Amanda and I go back a long way. We were at primary school together. I felt sad about the way things turned out…"

In the darkness, she couldn't make out the expression on his face. She didn't have to. His voice was as sharp as a shard of glass. This had been a big mistake.

"I'm not buying it. You're a gold-digger and, if you think that you can show up here and see if there are any nuggets for the taking, then you can think again."

"How dare you?"

"Let's not go down that road, Rosie. You and I both know exactly how I dare. I should have known better than to expect anything else from a semi-clad waitress I happened to meet at a cocktail bar once upon a time."

Rosie saw red. Her hand flew up and she felt the sting of flesh meeting flesh as it hit his cheek, sending his head back. Before she could back away, he was holding her wrist, pulling her towards him until she could breathe in that uniquely masculine scent she had always found so intoxicating.

"If I were you, I wouldn't try that again."

"I'm sorry," she muttered, appalled at her lack of self-control and even more appalled at the way her body was reacting to the proximity of his. She tried to wriggle free of the steel band of his fingers around her wrist and just as suddenly as he had caught her hand, he released it to step back.

"I just don't appreciate being called a gold-digger. I'm not here to see what I can get from you, Angelo. You must think I'm crazy, to imagine for a second that I would—"

"Once an opportunist, always an opportunist."

"I've already told you that—"

"So you have. It's a well-worn road, Rosie, and not one I'm about to travel down again." His mouth twisted in a cynical half-smile. Even after all this time, and with enough loathing and bitterness towards the woman standing in front of him to sink a ship, Angelo still couldn't tear his eyes away from her face. Any more than he could have controlled his reaction when he had felt her supple body pressed up close against his.

"Angelo, I haven't come here to argue with you."

"Fine." He shrugged in a gesture that was exotically foreign and typically sexy.

From the very first instant she had laid eyes on him, Rosie had been bowled over. She had been working in London for over a year, serving drinks in an expensive club for well-heeled members, most of whom, she had clocked very early on, were married men either having illicit affairs or arranging to. Not even on the rough council estate where she had been brought up had she had to fend off so many unwanted advances.

It wasn't exactly what she had dreamt of when she had left behind her life of no hope and limited chances. Growing up, she'd had big plans to work in one of the high-class restaurants, starting from the bottom and working her way up and into the catering side of it. She loved cooking. She was good at it. But the high-class restaurants had all knocked her back. *Do you have any qualifications? Have you been to any cookery schools? No? Well…sorry. Don't call us, we'll call you if anything comes up…*

So she had ended up dressed in skimpy clothing, serving over-priced drinks to overweight businessmen. Her incredible looks had assured her a generous income and what choice had she had? She'd needed the money. And then, one night, dead on her feet, she had looked across the room and there he was—Angelo Di Capua. Six-foot-four of pure, unadulterated alpha male surrounded by six well-dressed businessmen, wearing a bored expression on his face. Had she but known it at the time, that was the very instant her fate had been sealed.

She surfaced from memory lane to find Angelo staring down at her with eyes that were as cold as the wind whipping through the layers of her clothes.

"You want to be civil?" Angelo shot her a curling smile

that sent shivers racing up and down her spine. "Let's play that game, then. What have you been up to for the past few years? Still trawling cocktail bars in search of wealthy men?"

"I never did that."

"So many things we disagree on." Yet it hadn't always been that way. Before everything had collapsed, he had considered her to be the best thing ever to have happened to him. Just thinking about it now made something deep inside him twist with pain.

"I…I haven't done any waitressing for a while," Rosie told him, determined to keep the conversation as remote and as polite as possible. She knew that what she should really be doing was leaving, walking away, but she couldn't fight the small cowardly part of her that wanted just a little bit longer in his company because, like it or not, such a big part of her was still wrapped up in him.

"In fact, I finished at catering college a couple of years ago and I've been cooking at one of the top restaurants in London ever since. It's hard work, but I enjoy it."

"I can't picture you behind the scenes. Nor can I picture you giving up a lucrative lifestyle of generous tips to take a pay cut."

Rosie flushed. "I don't care whether you can picture it or not. It's the truth. You know I always wanted to go into the food business."

"I stopped believing what I thought I knew about you a long time ago. But you're right. Who wants to waste time bickering over a piece of history that has little relevance now? Let's change the subject. Have you managed to net some poor guy? I can't imagine you'd still be single after all this time."

Angelo had no idea what possessed him to ask that question, but why fight the truth? It was something he had wondered about over the years. He didn't like himself for his curiosity, not about a woman he had so thoroughly eliminated from his life. But, like some low-level virus, the question had circulated in his bloodstream, pernicious and resistant to the passage of time.

Rosie stilled. She could feel the sudden grip of clammy perspiration.

"I'm still single." She tried to laugh but there was a nervous edge to her laughter.

Angelo looked at her narrowly, head tilted to one side. He hadn't seen her for years, yet it seemed that he could still tune in to the nuances in her voice, the slight pauses and small hesitations that were always a clue as to what was going through her head. So there was a man in her life. His lips thinned as the silence hummed between them, broken only by the hushed voices of the people waiting to enter the crematorium.

"Now, why is it that I don't quite believe that?" he asked softly. "Why lie, Rosie? Do you think I care one way or the other what's going on in your life?"

"I know you don't. And it's none of your business whether I have someone in my life or not." She was tempted to tell him about Ian, to pretend that there was someone significant in her life, but she couldn't bring herself to lie. In fact, just the thought of Ian made her feel a little ill.

"I should go," she said with a hint of desperation. She took a couple of steps back and nearly stumbled. She was no longer accustomed to wearing heels.

"Good idea," Angelo said smoothly. "And then we can put an end to this charade of pretending that we're actually interested in each other's lives." He turned away abruptly, but couldn't walk away because the group who had attended the cremation, now standing outside, was splintering apart.

Rosie guessed that they would be making their separate ways to whatever pub they intended to go to. She saw Lizzy give her a little wave and wondered what the other woman must be thinking—that a friend had rolled up and after a three-year absence had shown surface interest before disappearing outside with the husband of the deceased.

She had barely paid attention to any of the other people there, but now she could recognise that a short, rotund man bearing down on them had also been there in the front row and she forced herself to stand her ground. As did Angelo, although once again she saw him glance at his watch.

She wondered what their marriage had been like. She had walked away and never looked back. Had they been happy? She couldn't think so, but who knew?

"Foreman."

Angelo greeted the man curtly before reluctantly turning around to make introductions.

It seemed that James Foreman was a lawyer.

"Nothing big and fancy." James extended his hand out to Rosie. "Small practice near Twickenham. Brr, cold out here, isn't it? Still, what can you expect in the middle of February?" He seemed to suddenly remember that he was at a funeral and altered his tone accordingly. "Terrible shame, all this. Terrible shame."

"Miss Tom is in a bit of a rush, Foreman."

Rosie nodded awkwardly. "I'm afraid I won't be able to make it to the pub—one of Amanda's friends mentioned that everyone would be gathering there to pay their respects. I've travelled all the way from East London and I really need to be getting along."

"Of course, of course! But I need to corral the pair of you for a word." James Foreman looked around him with a little frown, as though searching for somewhere convenient into which the corralling could take place. Rosie, by now, was thoroughly confused. More than anything else, she wanted to be gone. It had been a mistake seeing Angelo again. That part of her life was a chapter that should be firmly closed. Coming here had reopened it and now she knew that their brief, embittered encounter would prey on her mind for weeks ahead.

"What's this about, Foreman?" Angelo asked in a clipped voice.

"Stroke of luck finding you both here. Of course, Mr Di Capua, I knew that you would be here but... Well, put it this way, Miss Tom, it's saved me a bit of bother tracking you down...not that it would have been difficult. All part of the business."

"Cut to the chase, Foreman."

"It's about a will."

Rosie had no idea what this had to do with her. She did know, however, that the longer she stood still the colder it felt. She glanced across to Angelo, her eyes drawn to the harsh, beautiful lines of his face like the unerring and dangerous tug of a moth towards an open flame.

The last conversation they had ever had was imprinted on her brain. The coldness in his eyes, the contempt in his voice when he had told her that he wanted nothing more to do with her. They had been dating for nearly a year, the most wonderful year of her entire life. She had not stopped marvelling at how this terrific, wealthy, sophisticated guy had pursued her. Later he had told her that the second he had laid eyes on her he had wanted her, and that he was a man who always got what he wanted. He had certainly got her and she had been on cloud nine.

Of course, on the home front, things had not been quite so rosy. Jack's problems had been deteriorating steadily and Amanda... How could she not have guessed that, whilst she had been waxing lyrical about the love of her life, her best friend had been busily storing up jealousy and resentments that would one day spill over into the horror story from which none of them had emerged intact?

While the past threatened to overwhelm her, James Foreman was still talking in a low voice, ushering them away from the chapel and towards the car park which was shrouded in darkness.

"Hang on a minute." Rosie stopped dead in her tracks and the other two men turned to look at her. "I don't know what's going on here and I don't care. I need to get back home."

"Have you been listening to a word Foreman's been saying?"

Actually, no, she hadn't. "So Amanda left a will. I don't see what that has to do with me. I haven't seen her for over three years." She looked apologetically at the lawyer who probably hadn't a clue what was going on. "We had a bit of a falling out, Mr Foreman. Amanda and I used to be friends, but something happened. I only came here because I felt sad about how things had ended between us."

"I know all about the falling out, my dear."

"Do you? How?"

"Your friend—"

"Ex-friend."

"Your ex-friend was a very vulnerable and confused young woman. She came to see me when…eh…she was having certain difficulties…"

"Difficulties? What difficulties?" Rosie laughed bitterly. Mandy had played her cards right and she had got exactly what she had wanted—Angelo Di Capua. "All's fair in love and war," she had once said to Rosie when they were fifteen. Rosie had come to see just how tightly her so-called friend had been prepared to cling to that outlook.

"Not for me to say at this juncture. Look, why don't we

nip to a little bistro I know not far from here? It should be relatively quiet at this hour and it would save you both the hassle of coming to my office in the morning. My car's in the car park so we could go right now. Mr Di Capua, perhaps your driver could come and collect you in an hour or so?"

They were virtually at his car and Rosie heard Angelo click his tongue impatiently but he shrugged and made a brief phone call before sliding into the passenger seat, leaving her to clamber in the back. She felt as though she had no choice but to surrender to this turn of events. The short drive was completed in silence and twenty minutes later they were in a bistro which, as James Foreman had predicted, was fairly empty.

"I find it hard to believe that Amanda would leave a will," Angelo said the second they were seated. "She had no one in her life. At least, no one of any significance."

"You'd be surprised," James Foreman murmured, his sharp eyes flicking between them.

"What were the difficulties you were talking about?" Rosie pressed. Next to her, Angelo's hand, resting on the table, brought back sharp memories of how things had once been between them, cutting through the bitterness, leaving her dry-mouthed and panicked.

"Your friend was an emotional young woman carrying burdens she found difficult to cope with. She came to see me about a certain property she owned. I believe you know the property I'm talking about, Mr Di Capua—a certain cottage in Cornwall?" He turned to Rosie with a warmly sympathetic half-smile. "I understand the problems you both had. Over the years I built up a strong rapport with your friend. She was a needy soul and I became something of a father figure for her. My wife and I had her over many times for dinner. Indeed, we both did our best to counsel her on—"

"Are we ever destined to get to the point, Foreman?"

"The point is that the cottage was your wife's prized possession, Mr Di Capua. She found refuge there."

"Refuge from what?" Rosie interjected. She glanced across to Angelo's hard, uncompromising profile and saw him flush darkly.

"We're not here to discuss the state of my marriage," Angelo bit out, meeting her puzzled stare with ice-cold eyes. "So she went a lot to the cottage." He dragged his eyes away from her face. Hell, how was it that she could claw a reaction out of him? Was it possible that only this burning hatred could find a response in him?

"And the cottage belonged to her. In its entirety. Along with the acreage surrounding it. You recall, Mr Di Capua, she insisted shortly after you were married that you give it to her so that she could feel secure there and could be certain that it would never be taken away."

"I recall," Angelo said abruptly. "I agreed because I owned the estate alongside it. I could keep an eye on her."

"Keep an eye on her? Why would you want to do that, Angelo?"

"Because." Once again he looked at her. Once again he felt that surge of blistering, chaotic emotion which was a damn sight more than he had felt for the past few years. For as long as he could remember he had been completely dead inside. "Amanda had a problem with alcohol. She fancied the cottage because she wanted peace and quiet. On the other hand, with her fondness for the bottle, I couldn't let her stay there without some form of supervision. She was unaware that I owned the estate abutting the cottage. I always made sure that one of my people was around to check on her now and again."

"I can't believe she started drinking. She was always so sure she wouldn't go down that road."

"Is that your convoluted way of asking me whether I drove her to drink?"

"Of course not!"

"Because you're not sitting here at my request. Nor are you entitled to any explanations or niceties from me. You burned your bridges three years ago and lost the right to have a voice, as far as I am concerned."

Rosie flushed bright red. She forgot that they both had an audience. The only person she was aware of was Angelo, looking at her with deep, dark hostility.

"You forget that I don't even *want* to be here. Why should I? Why would I want to spend more time than absolutely necessary in your company?"

James Foreman cleared his throat and Angelo was the first to break the stranglehold of their stares.

"The cottage," he said curtly. "Cut to the chase, man, and get on with it."

"She left the cottage to you, Miss Tom."

"Don't be ridiculous!" Angelo cut in before Rosie had had time to assimilate what had been said to her. He placed both hands squarely on the table and leant forward, his body language bristling with intimidation, and the lawyer looked back at him with an apologetic smile.

"It's all above board, Mr Di Capua. Amanda left the cottage to her friend."

"Why on earth would she do that?" Rosie asked in bewilderment.

"Before you start getting any ideas," Angelo gritted, looking at her, "over my dead body will you so much as put a foot over the threshold of that place." He sat back and turned to stare at the lawyer who, for someone round-faced and sheepishly polite, was doing a good job of not being in the slightest bit cowed by a toweringly angry Angelo. A lesser man would have run for the hills at this point.

"I'm very much afraid that there's very little you can do to prevent Miss Tom from accepting what has been willed to her," James Foreman said, in the same apologetic voice. He looked at her with kindly eyes. "Whatever happened between you, my dear, there were regrets."

"I wouldn't dream of accepting anything Amanda may have left to me, Mr Foreman."

"Well, hallelujah!" Angelo flung his hands up in a gesture of pure satisfaction, success rightfully accepted as his due. "So for once, we're singing from the same song sheet. Now that this little charade is over, perhaps you two can get together and work out the paperwork to ensure that Miss Tom relinquishes whatever dodgy hold she may think she has on my property—which, in point of fact, will be a matter of necessity because I intend to develop it within the year. Now, if that's all?"

"You always wanted to go into the catering business— am I right, Miss Tom?"

Rosie nodded dumbly. She felt as though she had been taken on a rollercoaster ride. Her thoughts were all over the place. Every part of her body was in a state of shock. All over again, and to her dismay, she was realising how powerfully Angelo Di Capua still affected her, despite her deep loathing of him.

"How did you know?"

"Amanda kept tabs on you without you realising it, I expect." He shrugged. "With the Internet and social networks, it's virtually impossible to remain anonymous these days. At any rate, you might want to think about what was behind this legacy to you. Of course, you must do what your heart tells you to do, but Amanda began cultivating the land around the cottage. There's quite a bit of it, if I'm not mistaken."

"This conversation is going nowhere!" Angelo insisted, making a slashing motion with his hand.

"It is my duty to explain the circumstances of this will," the lawyer murmured, still looking at Rosie. "Amanda made plans of how the land was to be laid out, and what would grow where."

"But she didn't know that she would… She couldn't possibly predict…"

"I think she knew, deep down, that she was not destined for a long life. I also think that she was working up the courage to contact you to give you the land. Fate got in the way."

"This is so much to take in," Rosie said, dazed. "Perhaps…perhaps I might just have a look at the cottage." If nothing else, to see whether she might get full closure at least by visiting the place her one-time friend had obviously come to regard as a haven. Perhaps, more than attending a service in a chapel, visiting that cottage would be a better way to pay her final respects.

"Yes." She made her mind up, although she didn't dare look across to where Angelo was sitting in a silence far more threatening than any words. "Yes. I think, Mr Foreman, I would very much like to see that cottage."

CHAPTER TWO

"YOU'RE WASTING YOUR time." Angelo rounded on her the second the lawyer had disappeared back to his car, into the night. "You surface here from out of nowhere and suddenly you think you're a cottage richer?"

Rosie looked up at him. He was one of the few men who towered above her when she was in heels. Once upon a time, that had made her feel very feminine and very protected. Now it made her feel intimidated.

"I don't think anything of the sort."

"No. Well, you moved very swiftly from wanting nothing to do with a dubious inheritance to informing us that you would be paying it a visit." His chauffeur-driven luxury car pulled up alongside them and, as she tried to turn in the direction of the station, Angelo stepped out in front of her, blocking her path.

"Not so fast," he said grimly.

"I need to get back."

"Really? To whom?"

"There's nothing to discuss, Angelo."

"There's a hell of a lot to discuss and we've only just begun. Get in the car." He pulled open the car door and moved around so that he was now somehow cornering her into stepping into the long, powerful car. It remained gently purring while George, the guy with whom she had laughed on many an occasion in the past, stared straight ahead with a blank expression.

Their eyes locked and Rosie was the first to look away, ducking into the car with a jerky shrug of her shoulders.

"Address. Where do you live?"

"There's no need to put yourself out. I'm fine being dropped to the station."

"You haven't answered my question."

Rosie snapped out her address and leant back in the car seat while Angelo relayed the information to his driver before sliding shut the partition between them. She could feel heat racing through her body like a raging fever and, although her voice was controlled, that was about the only thing that was. Her heart was beating like a jackhammer and she was struggling to string her thoughts together.

Here she was, back in this car with him! Except the good old days were now lost in the mists of time, replaced with a present that bristled with threat.

"So," Angelo drawled. "Drop the protestations of innocence. We know each other too well. Did you know about any of this before you came here? I never thought that you had anything further to do with Amanda after you left, but maybe I was wrong."

"No, I most certainly did *not* know about any cottage! And Mandy and I have not been in contact since… Well, since…" She looked away, briefly unable to speak as the circumstances of the past reared up, threatening to devour her.

She remembered the horror of the last time she and Angelo had met, when she had turned up longing to see him, excited as always, because the short periods they spent apart had always felt like an eternity. He had opened the door to her and she had known immediately that something was wrong. Her smile had faltered and she had stood there in the doorway of his amazing house in Chelsea, no longer a welcome visitor, his lover, but someone to be dispatched. She had known it before he had even uttered a word.

And, actually, he had said remarkably little. There had been no need. He had just held out all those damning little tickets, receipts from the pawnbrokers, and she had known exactly what was happening.

Their glorious relationship had terminated with him believing her to be a cheap, worthless gold-digger who had conned him out of huge sums of money, for he had been a generous lover. He had seen the evidence of her greed in the proof of items of jewellery she had sold. Evidence that had been supplied by her one-time best friend and used against her.

Was it any surprise that he was staring at her as though she was something that had crawled out from under a rock, asking her whether she had known about the existence of a cottage that might be worth something?

Rosie took a deep breath. It made her feel giddy.

"It's not going to happen," he informed her coldly. "You. The cottage. Forget it. Look at me when I'm talking to you."

"You have no right to boss me about." But she did look at him. Thrown into shadow, his face was all menacing angles and planes.

"Amanda and I were not divorced at the time of her death. I will fight you through the courts if you try and get your greedy little paws on so much as a square inch of that place."

"I never said that I was going to…" But a cottage, out in the country, away from the daily grind of the city; away from Ian, a man she had met once six months previously when she had decided that enough was enough, that it was time to try and join the ranks of the living… A man who had refused to take no for an answer, who had tried to force himself on her, who had become a silent, scary stalker.

A bolt hole away from it all suddenly presented itself to her like manna from heaven.

"Then why don't you try and justify your sudden decision to check it out?"

"Maybe I think it might be the place to say goodbye to Mandy," Rosie told him painfully, and he burst out laughing again, just as he had when they had been standing inside the chapel at the crematorium.

"So suddenly you're all bleeding heart and flowers?"

"Why does it matter so much to you whether I go to that cottage or not? Why does it matter if I decide that it might be somewhere I could live?" Rosie asked.

"It sits on my grounds."

"Mr Foreman said that it had some land, that Mandy had been cultivating it."

"Ah, so your little ears had already pricked up even while you were mouthing all the right platitudes about wanting nothing from Amanda." What else could he expect? The woman looked like an angel and spoke in a soft voice that reeked of milk and honey, and all things good, and yet didn't he know better? He let his eyes rove over her body. Her coat was open and he could make out a stretchy black dress underneath. He had instant recall of the length of her limbs, entwined with his, as pale as his were brown; her small breasts which she'd used to complain about laughingly but which were perfect, the perfect handful, the perfect mouthful...

He yanked himself back from the brink of memories that had no place whatsoever in his life.

"If Mandy left me that cottage with the land, then why shouldn't I take it?" Rosie was spurred into demanding.

"At last. A bit of honesty. I can deal with that. It's so

much healthier than the sad face and the honeyed words. If that will is as watertight as Foreman implies, then you'll be amply recompensed for letting it go. And, as we both know, money talks as far as you are concerned." He delivered a chilling smile.

What would he say if she decided to retaliate? Rosie wondered. But she knew that she would never do that. Maybe there was just that part of her that wouldn't be able to deal with the ugliness of the truth, with the fact that, whilst he had been seeing her, he had also been seeing Mandy. Maybe that was something she would never, ever want him to confirm. There was such a thing as too much truth.

"It's why I told him about all that stuff you flogged," Mandy had said when challenged. "He was looking for an excuse to break up with you so I gave him one and he took it. Didn't think twice, in fact! More fool you for thinking that he was your knight in shining armour. People like us don't get knights in shining armour, Rosie. People like me and you and Jack live off the scraps. Angelo was just another guy stringing you along while giving me the come-on behind your back. You should thank me for getting rid of him for you. You'd never have been tough enough to handle him."

And how could Rosie not believe her when, a month later, there had been a wedding? She had heard it on the grapevine.

So did she want to start a tit-for-tat fight now? Did she want to hear him tell her exactly how little she had meant to him? The past was the past and re-opening old wounds was only going to hurt *her*. Angelo would be just fine.

And, if he never knew where that money had gone, then so be it. That too was a story wrapped up in guilt and not one she wanted to discuss.

"What do you mean?"

"I mean I'll pay you off," Angelo intoned harshly. For a few seconds he had lost her. When they had been lovers, he had interpreted those fleeting moments of withdrawal when her eyes had clouded over as flashes of vulnerability. He had made it his mission to wait them out until she could tell him for herself where she had gone. Now he knew the answer. She hadn't been so much dealing with some internal tussle, which she'd had yet to confide, as calculating how much she could screw him for. Doing the maths in her head. Indulging in a bit of mental arithmetic involving his money and all those expensive items of jewellery he had lavished on her.

Angelo didn't come from money. He'd got there the hard way, working like a beast at school, a small backwater school in Italy where it wasn't cool to get good grades. He'd lucked out when, at the age of sixteen, he had managed to win a scholarship to study abroad.

His mother had urged him to take it. He was her only son and she had wanted nothing more than for him to succeed. She'd worked in a shop and as a cleaner on two evenings a week. Did he want to end up scraping the barrel like her? He had grabbed the opportunity with both hands and had challenged any one of those rich, private-school kids to look down on him. He had made sure to stay focused and had realised that to get on he had to do one better than everyone else. He had to go the extra mile. He had. And he had at university. The price had been steep, for during that period his mother had died and he had not been there for her.

He had reasoned that life's experiences made you tough. He was a rock, alone in the world and determined to master it as a legacy to his mother. He wasn't one of those gullible kids born with a silver spoon in their mouth. He couldn't be taken in by a pretty face. Except he had been, and just thinking about it made him see red. Rosie Tom had got to him in a way no other woman ever had. Hell, she had made him start revising his priorities.

"I can have people in tomorrow evaluating its worth and I can get a cheque to you the day after."

"Is it because it's of sentimental value?" Rosie hazarded.

"No idea what you're talking about."

"Do you feel attached to the place because it was somewhere she loved? I know that sometimes a person can feel helpless when dealing with someone who has a drinking problem."

"Three years away and you really and truly imagine yourself as an amateur psychologist. Stick to the catering, Rosie, or the cooking, or whatever else it is you do." Did she really think that he would ever fall for that sympathetic, butter-wouldn't-melt-in-the-mouth routine again?

Rosie flushed. "I don't imagine myself as anything of the sort. I was just curious as to…"

"As to what happened once you exited the stage and the curtain fell?" He looked at her narrowly. "I really wouldn't bother trying to fish for information. Just tell me when you intend to go to the cottage."

"Why do you ask?" So there weren't going to be any confidences. This was the tenor of whatever remained between them: bitterness and dislike. Well, that would make things easier, she told herself, but it still hurt to think how far they had both come from where they had once been.

"Because I intend to make sure that I'm there at the same time."

"What for?" Rosie's mouth dropped open as she contemplated seeing him again, having all these emotions churned up anew. "I can let you have my decision one way or another via Mr Foreman. If I decide that I don't want the place, then I'm sure he'll be the first to let you know. Or maybe," she added with acerbity, "you want to make sure that there's nothing there that doesn't belong to *you*."

"I actually hadn't considered that possibility but, now that you've mentioned it, it's certainly one worth thinking about." The journey had passed without him even noticing. Now they were in front of a terraced house that was claustrophobically hemmed in by a sprawl of identical terraced houses on either side of it. In the depths of winter, there was nothing whatsoever charming about it, and he thought that even in the height of summer it would still proudly announce its mediocrity.

"That's an awful thing to say."

"Oh well, if the cap fits…" The car had pulled to a stop, smoothly pulling in to a vacant spot right in front of the house. "I see investment wasn't part of the grand plan when you pawned the jewellery," he observed. "Because I can't imagine that this place will ever get to the elevated status of the up-and-coming." Rosie flushed and paused midway to opening the car door.

"I don't own this, I rent it, and I would rather if we didn't dwell on the past. I mean, it's over and done with and we've both moved on." She thought about Jack and the guilt that had followed her around for such a long time. She hadn't hesitated in pawning those items of jewellery even though, in another place and another time, the thought of selling things given to her by the man she had fallen in love with would have been abhorrent. In a place and time where her conscience was clear.

She knew that Angelo despised her for what she had done. How much more would he have despised her if he had known the full story?

"So, in other words, the cottage really would be a fantastic opportunity for you—no rent to pay, no mortgage to cover. I'm not surprised that you're desperate to put the past to bed."

Rosie looked at him, sprawled indolently against the car door, a lurking, dangerous predator having fun with the prey that had once escaped him. She got the feeling that he would be happy to maul her should she make one wrong move. And expressing interest in a cottage he considered his definitely fell into that category.

Whatever had gone wrong in his marriage—and she was certain that something had somewhere along the way, for why else would Amanda have taken to the bottle?— here they now were and the past certainly had not been forgotten.

"I just want to have a look at it."

"Like I said, I'll expect you to inform me the instant you decide to go there. I'm going to give you my private number. Use it."

"And if I choose not to?" Rosie dared.

"Word of advice—don't even think of going down that road."

Rosie spent the next week seriously wondering whether she should just leave well alone. James Foreman had been in touch again, had wanted to find out what she intended to do. There were all sorts of papers that required signing. She would need to see him; he could arrange a meeting. There were things he needed to discuss with her.

Still tense and preoccupied after seeing Angelo and being subjected to the full force of his hatred, and still smarting from his warning to ditch any thoughts of actually taking up the legacy that had been deposited at her doorstep, Rosie deferred any meeting. She honestly no longer knew what she should do. London had not turned into the stuff of dreams, but it was home, for better or for worse. Could she sacrifice it on a whim, because she was in a difficult situation at the moment? Difficult situations didn't last for ever.

And how ethical would it be to accept something from a woman she had spent the past three years trying to forget? How hypocritical to imagine that she could conveniently overlook the dire circumstances of their broken friendship to take what was on offer because it suited her? Her lawyer had hinted at Amanda's regrets but could accepting a guilt gift ever be justified?

In the end, Ian made up her mind for her. Just as he had been the reason for her considering the cottage in the first place.

The calls from him, containing barely veiled threats. The bombardment of text messages...

Rosie had been to the police ages ago to be told that nothing could be done. A crime had yet to be committed. With no chance of an injunction being issued against him, Rosie battened down the hatches and tried to ignore his attempts to intrude into her life. She wasn't a kid. She was an adult. She could deal with a loser who couldn't take no for an answer. She had dealt with far worse growing up! He was no match for any of those creeps who had tried to make her life hell on the grim council estate where she had grown up. Being attractive had never worked to her advantage. But she found that she could deal with wolf-whistles and boys circling her on their bikes and trying to get her to go out with them.

And she could almost deal with the hang ups and the text messages from Ian. But, returning to her house on the Friday two weeks after that eventful funeral, Rosie unlocked the front door, entered the house and knew instantly that something was wrong.

It was very late and the lights had all been switched off.

It was the first thing to alert her to the notion that someone was either inside the house or had been inside the house. She always left the light in the hall on during the winter; it lent the illusion of homeliness and dispelled the reality of a place that was as inviting and welcoming as a prison.

With one hand on her mobile, she silently scoured the property, which wasn't large. Just three rooms downstairs, including the kitchen, and one bedroom upstairs with a bathroom adjoining it. At the first sign of an intruder, she would not have hesitated to call the police but, having re-assured herself that the place was empty, she soon dis-covered that there was no room to breathe a sigh of relief because someone had certainly been to the house and it hadn't taken her long to find out their identity.

Propped up against the toaster in the kitchen, Ian had left a note warmly telling her how wonderful it was finally to get to see the inside of her house and informing her that he hoped to be back soon, perhaps when she was there so that they could try and sort out their silly differences.

Heart beating fast, Rosie scrolled down the address book in her phone and found what she was looking for. She didn't think twice. Was that because old habits died hard? Once upon a time, Angelo had been her rock. He was now her sworn enemy but was there still some lin-gering feeling lurking deep inside her that she could still depend on him if she was threatened? Was her lack of hesitation some left-over, unconscious emotion that she couldn't quantify or explain?

Angelo answered on the second ring. He knew instantly who the caller was. He had given her his mobile number and she had grudgingly returned the favour by giving him hers. What choice had she had? Like it or not, with a cot-tage in the equation, there might be the need to commu-nicate with him.

It was after ten-thirty at night, but he was still working, albeit in his sprawling London house. At the sight of her name on his phone, Angelo pushed himself away from his desk and swivelled his chair towards the impressive abstract painting which dominated most of one wall of the massive downstairs room which he had had converted into a study. He had paid a ridiculously large sum of money for it, but he couldn't remember the last time he had given it a second glance.

He realised that he had been expecting her phone call for some time. In fact, he had anticipated her getting in touch pretty much as soon as they had parted company. One gold-digger living in a dump meets one freebie cottage in its own grounds in a beautiful part of the country and, hey presto, what else could follow but a rapid response? He'd found, as the days had passed, that he had been looking forwards to hearing her flimsy justification for grabbing what had landed in her lap. Indeed, he had been grimly looking forwards to the pleasurable prospect of ensuring that she didn't get her hands on what she so clearly wanted. If it meant paying her off, then he looked forwards to handing her a cheque, while ramming home his scathing views on opportunists.

"Well, if it isn't Rosie Tom," he drawled, eyes on the painting, although he wasn't actually seeing the slashing lines and curious splashes of paint on canvas. What he was seeing was the perfection of a heart-shaped face; a full mouth that always looked as though, given the right provocation, it would part in a brilliant smile; eyes that made something soften inside him, a body that had once driven him mad with desire.

"I'm really sorry if I'm disturbing you. I know it's Friday and you're probably out…"

Angelo decided that she was less than entitled to any

clue as to his whereabouts. "Before you continue wasting time with a long, pointless spiel, just tell me what you want to say. Or rather, shall I tell you what you want to say? Save you the bother? You've had a good, long think and you've decided that you just can't resist the pull of something for nothing."

"I…" She thought about Ian finding his way into the house. There was no burglar alarm and little chance that her cheapskate landlord would ever run to one. Her voice wobbled and she took a deep breath, trying to steady her nerves, but like someone suddenly feeling the aftershock of some terrible disaster her body began to tremble and she had to sit down on the cheap sofa.

Lounging back, Angelo stiffened, sat up straight and frowned. Was she all right? For a second there, he could have sworn that she was going to burst into tears. He reminded himself that this was the woman who had successfully pulled the wool over his eyes for months.

"It's late, Rosie, and I'm busy. So why don't you just get to the point? Am I right?"

"I'm going to see if I can get through to Mr Foreman tomorrow. I'm sure he won't mind letting me have the key to the cottage. I…I…" Once again her voice nearly broke and she had to inhale deeply to gather herself.

"What's going on with you, Rosie?"

"What do you mean? I don't know what you're talking about."

"Why ring now? Isn't this a phone call that could have waited until morning?"

"I'm sorry. I've had a bit of a fright… I wasn't thinking straight. You're right, of course, I should have waited to call you at a more convenient hour. It's not as though I can go knocking on Mr Foreman's door at this hour of the night. Look, forget I called. When I get through to the lawyer and I sort the keys out, I'll call you. I know you have a vested interest in the place, and after everything I'm fine with you wanting to be there just in case I find something valuable that isn't part of that stupid will."

"What fright?" He fought down an urgent need to see her face. He had always been able to tell what was going on in her head from her face, her eyes. It dawned on him that that was a talent he might well have lost.

"It's nothing. Well, nothing I can't handle."

"Not good enough. Explain."

"Why should I? It's none of your business what's going on in my life at the moment!" And she would do well to remember that. She had rushed to the phone because some primitive instinct had taken over. One meeting with him and here she was, already acting like a complete idiot!

Angelo Di Capua was the last person whose voice she should want to hear in a time of crisis. Jack would have been more than happy to listen to her babble on about the crazy guy she had dated once. He would have offered to come over the second she told him that Ian had broken in. He knew all about Ian. But had she called him? No. Instead, her brain had gone on temporary leave and some insane instinct had taken over. Honestly. How lame was the excuse of the cottage when it came to phoning him?

"Expect me to be at the cottage some time over the weekend. Probably Sunday. If you want to be there, then fine. I can't tell you where you can or can't be, although if it's my cottage then technically you'd be trespassing." She covered her show of weakness for calling him in the first place with a virulent diatribe which didn't make her feel any better.

"Ah, that's more like it. Out come the claws. Have you been on the Internet to find out how much you could get for it?"

"Goodbye, Angelo. I'll see you when I see you."

She should have phoned Jack. Jack, who along with Amanda had packed up his belongings and fled their council estate just outside Liverpool before they had become too old or too resigned to fight the "no way out" signs. Amanda might have turned traitor, selling her friend down the river for the chance of netting Angelo, but Jack had always remained her best friend through thick and thin. Why hadn't she called him instead of Angelo? Even though he was all loved up with his partner, Brian, a doctor at one of the big London hospitals, he would have jumped in his little car without hesitation and stayed with her until she had talked herself out of her anxiousness.

As things stood, she spent a wakeful night, listening out for noises, wondering how Ian had managed to infiltrate her haven. He didn't have a key. She had gone out with the man once. But he must have followed her at some point to know where she lived. She shuddered thinking about it. She wondered whether there was any point contacting the police. Would they be able to do anything? Or would they say, again, that no crime had been committed? They might even doubt her when she told them that there was no way that Ian could have a key to her house.

During the course of her restless night, the idea of fleeing to the countryside seemed to make more and more sense. She would have to give notice at the restaurant, but there was a chance that they would release her if she explained the situation. She was on good terms with the head chef who ran the show.

The following morning, she rang James Foreman as early as she thought acceptable and told him that she had decided to take a look at the cottage as soon as possible.

"Today if I can," she said, walking through the house and flinging bits and pieces of clothing into her holdall.

"I know it's very last minute, and I should have called you earlier, but I just decided on the spur of the moment."

Excellent idea, the lawyer told her. She could come to his house for the keys, although of course Angelo had a set of his own.

"I'll come to you," Rosie said hastily. "I promised Mr Di Capua that I would let him know if I intended visiting the cottage and I have. I spoke to him yesterday. Of course, you might want to confirm that with him yourself. No rush there, though," she continued vaguely. "I gather that he's a very busy man. I'm sure he wouldn't be interested in dashing down to Cornwall on a weekend."

By the time the phone call had ended, a time had been arranged for her to collect the key. Having made her mind up, she couldn't wait to go.

"I'm going to do it." She called Jack on her mobile to tell him as she locked the front door behind her and stuck out her hand for a cab. "Long story, but I don't feel safe in the house any more. I know Ian's harmless, but it's still a little scary to think…well…"

Jack did as she expected him to, spoke to her in that soothing voice of his, told her that it was a good idea and that she shouldn't feel guilty about accepting Mandy's gift because it was the least she could have done.

"She wrecked your life," he said, indignant, and as always fiercely loyal.

"Or else made me see Angelo for what he really was. Just a ship passing in the night. He never loved me, Jack, or else he wouldn't have been unfaithful behind my back with my best friend." Yet, seeing him again, he still got to her, still fired her up and made every pore and nerve-ending in her body rush into immediate red-alert mode.

There was nothing Jack could say to that, nothing that he had ever been able to say to that. They had talked about it endlessly in the weeks after the relationship had crashed and burned, until Rosie had become aware that she was boring her friend to death. At which point she stopped, and the only conversations she had on the subject were in her head.

"She did me a favour." Rosie thought of the glittering hatred in Angelo's eyes, those fabulous moss-green eyes that were so sexy and so unusual in someone of his exotically dark colouring.

"He should have heard you out about those pawn tickets, Rosie baby."

"Why would he? He didn't care enough to hear my side of the story. He was already moving on. No, he had *already* moved on." She was ashamed when she remembered how willing she would have been to force Angelo to hear her out, how happily she would have sacrificed her self-respect and begged for him to believe her. But in the end there had been no point, because he had married Amanda.

She felt drained and exhausted just thinking about it. She couldn't believe that he was now back in her life, determined to make her suffer in whatever way he could.

Forty minutes later, with the key to the cottage in her purse, Rosie wondered whether she had the strength to fight Angelo for a cottage she hadn't even seen and might well hate on sight. Of the three of them, Mandy had always been the one most determined to blank out the past and recreate it as something it had never been. The second she had met Angelo and sussed his wealth, she had hissed to Rosie that she should keep their background under wraps.

"A guy like that who could have anyone, literally anyone, would dump you in a heartbeat if he ever found out that you, me and Jack are refugees from a disgusting council estate up north. Can you imagine what he'd think if he knew that your dad died a drunk? That your best friend's mum was a junkie doing time? You wouldn't see him for dust."

Rosie had laughed. She wasn't ashamed of her background, even though she had wanted to escape it as badly as the other two. But, in all events, Angelo hadn't been the sort of guy who had wanted to quiz her about where she had grown up, nor had he confided in her about his own background, save to say that he had no brothers or sisters and came from a little village in Italy. They had laughed and made love and lived purely for the moment, and she had forgotten that they came from two different worlds because he had made her feel like a princess.

She splashed out on her train ticket and felt the thud of excitement as the train slowly lurched out of Paddington station. She'd had to wait a couple of hours at the station, not having booked her ticket in advance, but she hadn't minded. She had enjoyed sitting in one of the cafés, sipping coffee and watching the world go by.

The key in her bag felt like a good-luck charm and she had to resist the temptation to wrap her fingers around it.

She had to stop herself from grinning. She didn't care if Angelo loathed her and wanted to buy her out of this inheritance. This was her wonderful adventure and it couldn't have come at a more opportune time. She would grab it with both hands. Jack was right—why shouldn't she? Amanda had taken a shotgun to her life and blown it apart so maybe James Foreman was right. Maybe this was her way of making amends.

She felt a shadow of apprehension when she remembered that Angelo owned the grounds alongside it, but she would just have to work out how that might affect her. They had nothing to say to one another. Once he had accepted that he couldn't fling her off her own premises or buy her off, he would wash his hands of her. Hadn't he said something about wanting to develop the place anyway? He could develop his own land, turn it into whatever he wanted, and when that happened he would once again disappear from her life. It wasn't as though he would be finding excuses to show up on her doorstep. The opposite.

She sat back, closed her eyes and did her utmost to block the image of Angelo burning into her retina, tall, dark, dangerous and seeking some sort of revenge.

CHAPTER THREE

NOTHING COULD HAVE prepared Rosie for the picture-postcard cottage she walked into.

She had alternately dozed on the journey and speculated on what would be waiting for her at the end of it. She hadn't realised how stressed out she had been for the past few months, how accustomed she had become to looking over her shoulder, but the more distance she put between herself and London the more relaxed she became.

Her hours at the restaurant were insane. Eager to pack in as much experience as she possibly could, she worked like a demon and, on weekends, would obsessively try out variations on some of the dishes she had been taught to prepare, always trying to tweak them into something else, something that would give her the confidence to break away and do her own thing.

Her social life was practically nonexistent. She had become so used to it that it was only as she was travelling away from it that she could see how unhealthy a lifestyle it had become.

And then there was Ian, always hovering in the background like a bad dream. She had trained herself to ignore his invisible presence in her life and, at least until he had found a way into her house, she had firmly believed she had succeeded. Yet, as the train had eaten up the miles between London and Plymouth, she realised that she had been kidding herself. He had been just one more thing weighing her down and stressing her out.

But the second she stood in front of that cottage, all her problems seemed to magically disappear.

It wasn't a large cottage, but what it lacked in size it more than made up for in charm. Rosie had wondered how far away it would be from Angelo's house. She had wondered whether she would be able to see whatever mansion he owned towering in the distance, imposing an aura of permanent threat. She had known that, should that be the case, then she would never have been able to occupy it.

In fact, it was impossible even to guess that the cottage was anywhere near any other residence. It was set back from the main road, which was little more than a quiet country lane, and bordered by a white picket fence. Rosie had always imagined that white picket fences were things only found in kids' books. She was charmed by the reality of actually seeing one in the flesh and before even entering the cottage she spent a few minutes tracing the outline of it with her hand.

She imagined that in summer the little front garden would be a riot of colour and the apple trees on either side would be heavy with fruit. Behind the cottage, the land stretched away into fields and a copse.

It was idyllic. No wonder Angelo had reacted with rage and horror at the thought of her occupying it. Having fancied himself conned out of thousands by a conniving opportunist, he would have been seething at the prospect of her descending on what must be a very valuable slice of real estate which he considered belonged to him.

With a little sigh, Rosie let herself into the cottage. She didn't want to think about Angelo. She didn't want to think of him storming down to Cornwall and blazing a furious trail through her flimsy defences. She was still trying to recover from the blistering effect he had had on her two weeks ago when she had encountered him at the funeral. Now, she just wanted to luxuriate in the tranquillity of her surroundings and determine the direction of her life.

Inside the cottage was perfectly proportioned, but what captivated Rosie were the small touches that were all Amanda's: the choice of curtain, the choice of big and squashy sofas and the colour of the paint on the walls, rose-pinks and yellows.

She had wondered whether she would be spooked at walking into a house owned by her one-time friend, but she wasn't. She strolled from room to room and reflected that, whatever the outcome of Amanda's relationship with Angelo, she had managed to get what she had always dreamed of—a place close to the sea, decorated just the way she wanted, which was a style pinched from the occasional house magazine they used to drool over in their poky boxed houses on the council estate.

She didn't realise how long she had spent wandering through the cottage until her stomach began to rumble with hunger.

Of course, she hadn't thought to bring anything to eat with her. Fortunately, the fridge was completely empty. She didn't think she would have coped had there been proof of her friend there. Had the place been cleaned after Amanda had died? Rosie thought it might have been. Perhaps James Foreman had seen to that. He hadn't mentioned it, but he was just the sort of thoughtful, warm person who would have made sure the task was done in anticipation of her visiting.

She would have to go out, although without a car she had no idea how that would be achieved, and she was actively deliberating whether to call a taxi back or not when the doorbell rang.

Rosie froze instantly. It couldn't be Ian. Could it? She realised with dismay that thoughts of him were never too far away. Just in case, she tiptoed to the front door and quietly secured the chain before opening the door a crack.

Although it was only a little after five-thirty, it was already dark, a bottomless darkness quite unlike the darkness in London which was always punctuated with light from street lamps.

Whoever her caller was, he was standing to one side, just out of direct sight. Panic flared through her. She struggled for reason and told herself that there was no way that Ian could be standing outside her front door. It just wasn't possible! Yet, hadn't he found a way into her house in London? She wished she had thought to bring something heavy from the kitchen—a frying pan; a rolling pin. Something she could use as a weapon. Even as those thoughts flitted through her head, she was aware that she was over-reacting. She realised just how threatened she had felt by Ian over the months, even though she had stoutly told herself that she had nothing to fear from a guy who was two inches shorter than her and a very slight build.

"Well? Are you going to let me in, Rosie?" Angelo had not been to the cottage for a long time. In fact, he had only been there once, after he had allowed Amanda to have it, and then only to assess what renovations had needed doing. He had never been able to understand her reasons for demanding ownership when she had a perfectly good townhouse in London at her disposal, but then again he had never been one for the country life, despite owning his own country mansion. As investments went, it had served him well although he wouldn't have chosen to live there if he had had a gun to his head. It was there to appreciate in value and occasionally to host large events that were work-related. Three times a year, high-performing employees were treated to an all-expenses-paid weekend.

"What are you doing here?" Rosie marvelled that she could ever have imagined her caller to be Ian when the most obvious candidate was Angelo. Her irrational fear disappeared to be replaced by something else, a darker and more dangerous emotion that made her heart begin to beat erratically in her chest. He had stepped out of the shadows and she felt ridiculously overwhelmed by his tall, powerful presence.

"Didn't I tell you that I wanted to be here when you decided to have a look at your ill-gotten legacy?" He placed his hand flat against the door. In truth, there had been no need to rush down to Cornwall, but the second he had heard her voice down the end of the phone he had had no choice. It infuriated him.

"And why the latch?" he asked with silky sarcasm. "Left-over caution from having set up camp in a dump where it pays to make sure you know who your caller is before you open the door?"

"You should have told me that you would be coming." Rosie could hear the breathlessness in her voice, lurking just below the cool control she wanted to impose.

"Why, when the element of surprise is so much more enjoyable? Now, open the door, Rosie. I don't intend to spend the next hour having a conversation with you on the doorstep."

Reluctantly, Rosie unhooked the chain and opened the door, stepping aside so that he could brush past her into the hallway. She remained with her back pressed to the closed door, watching him warily as he looked around.

She had no idea what to say. She wondered what was going through his head. The woman he despised was standing in the hallway of a house that wasn't rightfully hers, given to her in the worst possible circumstances by someone who she hadn't set eyes on for three years. She couldn't drag her eyes away from his starkly handsome face and she flushed with embarrassment when eventually he finished his visual tour of the hallway and caught her staring at him.

"I think Mr Foreman must have arranged to have it all cleaned." Rosie rushed into speech whilst propelling herself away from the door towards the kitchen, simply because her legs felt too wobbly to maintain an upright position, even with the aid of the door to lean against.

"I did." Angelo hadn't known what to expect and he was surprised to find such muted colours and lack of personality. "I had my housekeeper for the main house bring a team in last weekend. Tell me, have you unpacked and settled in yet? You already look at home here, although maybe I'm being a little over-imaginative in thinking that it must be slightly strange walking around the house that once belonged to your friend. My mistake, your *ex*-friend. Or perhaps the *ex* makes it a little easier?" He sat on one of the kitchen chairs facing her and sprawled back, angling the chair so that he could stretch out his long legs, which he loosely crossed at the ankles.

At the funeral, she had been dressed in sombre colours as befitting a woman in so-called mourning. Now, she was back in casual attire, a pair of faded jeans, a loose, faded cotton sweater and trainers. She had always gone for the natural look and clearly nothing there had changed. He caught himself wondering whether she was wearing a bra and gritted his teeth together at his lapse in focus.

"I'm here to discuss relieving you of the property," Angelo drawled into the tense, lengthening silence. "I've spoken to Foreman and the will is sound. Unacceptable though I find it, you are the rightful owner of this place along with six acres of unmaintained land. Your ship's come in big time—no more toiling in a kitchen trying to make ends meet; no more pretending to enjoy getting hot and sweaty behind a stove while someone yells at you that you need to pick up speed and get your orders to the table." She still blushed. She was as tough as old boots and yet she still blushed. Amazing.

"I know you're probably going to be furious with me, Angelo, but I don't think I want to sell this cottage to you." She held her breath and waited for him to retaliate but he continued to sit there, lethally silent.

"And why would that be?" he asked softly.

Rosie shrugged and lowered her eyes. "I think it would do me good to leave London," she said truthfully. "I love my job but there are one or two things…happening."

"If you're trying to rouse my curiosity so that you can launch into a sob story, then you can forget it. Not interested. I have plans for this land and my plans don't include you living on it."

"If you had plans, then why didn't you approach Amanda for the land when she was alive? Why wait until now?"

Angelo was outraged that she dared even voice the question. It had been proven that the only thing she was interested in was money. Was she playing hardball in the hope that whatever financial deal he might offer could be upped? Or was she planning on sitting on the property until she was satisfied that it had reached its maximum value? To look at her no one would ever have guessed in a month of Sundays that she was capable of such cold-blooded calculation, yet he knew better.

"Amanda wanted this place. I gave it to her. It was not within my remit to try and wheedle it away from her for development. When it comes to you, however, the story is slightly different. And let's be honest here, Rosie, you can be bought. The only question is how much you're asking."

"I resent that."

"Don't make me laugh."

"Why are you still so bitter, Angelo?" She met his eyes and sustained his steady gaze even though she wanted to look away. "You married Mandy. It's not my fault your marriage didn't work out." She felt a rush of nerves as she overstepped the mark from polite conversation to uninvited opinion. "I'm sorry. It's none of my business." Restlessly, she stood up, went to the fridge and opened it, even though there was nothing there to find.

"I know what you think of me, Angelo. You think that you just have to throw money my way and I'll do whatever you want."

"Whatever I want?" A vivid image of her back in bed with him flashed through his head with startling clarity. He stood up, turned to her and Rosie gazed back at him with the suffocating feeling of being crowded.

What had that sibilant aside meant? Did he think that she was somehow offering herself to him?

"That's not what I meant."

"No? Sure about that?" He shoved his hands into his pockets and leant indolently against the fridge, barring her exit path to the kitchen door. The heightened atmosphere might be utterly inappropriate, but why kid himself? He was enjoying it. He was enjoying playing with the tantalising thought of having her, of seducing her into bed, of once again getting her so mindlessly turned on by him that she could scarcely breathe. He was suddenly so turned on that he could feel his arousal pushing insistently against the zip.

How could desire be so powerful that it could push past hatred to worm its own independent path?

He stepped aside, breaking the electric connection. Hell, what was going on here?

"Don't you have commitments to the people you work with?" Angelo drawled, giving himself sufficient physical space from her for his erection to subside. "Or do the commitments fall by the wayside when something better happens to come along?"

He strolled out of the kitchen and towards the small sitting room that overlooked the front garden. He knew that she was following him, although the rugs absorbed the sound of her footsteps.

"I have a very understanding boss," Rosie muttered helplessly. She hovered in the doorway, aware of how dangerous it was to get too close to him. For a second there in the kitchen, she had had a horrible feeling that if he had reached out and touched her, she would have melted, like wax in a hot flame. Did she have no pride or self-respect? Had she been giving off some crazy, subliminal signals that had encouraged him to think that she was still hot for him? Or had she imagined the whole surreal scenario— the lazy way he had looked at her, as though she could be his for the taking?

"I haven't had a chance—" she fought for composure and was pleased that she didn't sound as out of control as she felt "—to look outside—but if there's any chance that I could cultivate the land then I certainly will try and establish myself here. I know that my boss has a lot of contacts in this part of the world. I'm sure we would be able to work out a business proposition that would benefit both of us mutually." She couldn't read a thing in his brooding expression. She just knew that she couldn't let the messy past influence her now. The sooner she made her mind up, the quicker he would stop pursuing her in the hope of being able to buy her off. She couldn't deal with having him in the same space as her. After all this time, she was still far too vulnerable, even though she told herself that he was hateful, that she was over him, that he was the worst thing that had ever happened to her.

"So you'll have to give up trying to buy me off."

"And what happens if your optimistic prediction of a catering business doesn't materialise? This is your last chance to get your paws on a substantial amount of money. Turn it down now and it won't come your way again. Of course, you could always sell the house on the open market if it turns out that you need to, but times are tough even in this beauty spot. You could be sitting on bricks and mortar for months, with a floundering catering service and bailiffs banging on your door."

"Thanks very much for the vote of confidence, Angelo." There was a time when he would have backed her every inch of the way. She tore her mind away from that and focused on the image of Ian and the shadowy feelings of unease she had been living with for the past few months.

"And what about other commitments you might be leaving behind?" he murmured, his eyes roving lazily over her flushed face. He remembered that feeling he had got when he had asked her about her private life, that very slight pause before she answered. He found that he didn't much care for a boyfriend in the background, at least not while he was having hot fantasies about her.

"I guess I'll lose my deposit on the house. My landlord isn't the most sympathetic person in the world." Goodbye money she could ill afford, hello debt and a bank loan for a business which, as he had eloquently pointed out, could collapse around her, leaving her in a financial nightmare. She might have inherited a beautiful cottage and she might be intent on living in it, but she wasn't exactly bringing a great deal of disposable income with her to the table. She had managed to save a little, but how long would that last?

And what if Angelo decided to put a spoke in her wheel? He was rich, powerful, influential and he still hated her after all these years. Would he try and blow her out of the water because she had stubbornly refused to give in to him? Would he stoop that low? How steep was the price might she have to pay for running away from an awkward situation?

"I wasn't referring to your landlord and the small change you might owe him in a deposit."

"*You* might think that a few hundred pounds is small change, but it's not for me."

Angelo shot her a contemptuous, curling smile and refrained from telling her that she shouldn't have squandered the money she had taken from him. His initial reaction, on seeing her for the first time in three years at the funeral, and on hearing of the legacy that had been bequeathed to her, had been one of fury. He had not envisaged her living in the cottage. He would either fight her through the courts and wrench it out of her grasping hands, or he would fling sufficient money her way to make her disappear from his line of vision for good.

He hadn't banked on the unexpected, uninvited and one-hundred-percent untamed urgency of his physical response to her. Now, he wondered whether it might not be more satisfying to see her fail. He had never considered himself vengeful. Bitter, yes; angry, most definitely; but why waste time and energy on thoughts of revenge? And yet, the possibility of revenge now seemed to be landing neatly in his lap and he would be a saint not to yield to its temptation. Angelo knew for a fact that "saintly" was the last thing he was.

"Actually, I was referring to the man in your life," he

murmured with just the right hint of indifference in his voice.

Rosie wondered what he would say if she told him that she was running away from that particular man. Would it give him a sense of satisfaction? Would he give her a smug lecture on the wheel turning full circle for a woman like her?

"And, like I said to you before, my private life is none of your concern. James, Mr Foreman, tells me that there are a few legalities to go through before I move down here, but I intend to make the move as quickly as possible. I'm just telling you so that you don't think that you can try and work out a way of scaring me off."

"Is that what you think I'm doing? Scaring you off?"

"You know it is, Angelo. First you tell me that you'll pay to get rid of me, and then you tell me that if I don't agree to sell to you then any business idea I have is doomed to failure."

"And here I was thinking that I was being realistic." He wondered if the man she denied having in her life—or rather the man she wanted to keep a secret from him—was her boss. Maybe the guy was married, had kids. It was a distasteful thought and his lips thinned in immediate revulsion at the idea.

"I don't need you being realistic on my behalf," Rosie said coolly. "I'll take my chances."

"And if it turns out you need a rescue package? I don't suppose your parents will be able to pick up the pieces."

"I beg your pardon?" Rosie had no idea what he was talking about and she looked at him in bewilderment. "What parents?"

"The ones you have concealed up north somewhere. An accountant and a primary school teacher, if I'm not mistaken? You made sure never to mention their existence to me when we were going out, but then again, we didn't do much talking, did we?"

"We talked a lot." She looked at him and wondered whether he had deliberately demoted their relationship to a purely sexual one in an attempt to hurt her or whether she had misconstrued what they had meant to each other, reading too much into too little. "Who told you that my parents were a… What did you say? A teacher and an accountant?"

"Three guesses. No, you'd probably only need one. Amanda explained that you probably never talked about them because you were worried that I might find them too drab."

Rosie couldn't help herself. Even though her nerves were stretched to breaking point, she burst out laughing. She laughed until her eyes watered while Angelo stared at her, frowning with incomprehension.

"I would have been overjoyed to have had parents who were accountants or teachers," she finally said. "And I'm not surprised that Mandy made that story up." She felt a sudden burst of affection for the friend she had once had. "We used to long for normal parents."

Now it was Angelo's turn to be confused. He stilled as he sought to unravel the direction of her conversation, although he was half-distracted by the lingering smile on her face. "What are you talking about?"

"What did Mandy tell you about *her* parents?" Rosie asked curiously and Angelo's frown deepened. When had he lost control of the situation?

"There was nothing to tell," he said curtly. "She had none. She was raised by her grandmother who died a year before she moved to London. Where are you going with this?"

"I'm not the one who raised the topic," Rosie pointed out.

"Are you telling me that Amanda lied about her background? About yours?"

"I was raised by my father who was an alcoholic, Angelo, and I loved him. A lot. Even though he had a problem with his drinking. Even though he never came to a single parents' meeting or any sports event at school. Actually, even though he wasn't that bothered whether I went to school or not. Just for the record, I never played truant."

Angelo felt white-hot fury race through his bloodstream but he contained it. "So not only were you an opportunist," he gritted, "But you were also an out and out liar."

"I never lied!" But she hadn't been truthful either. She had lied by omission. Had she subconsciously worked out that Angelo would have discarded her like yesterday's garbage if he had known about her background? She had laughed when Amanda had warned her against telling him the truth about them, but had she secretly taken it on board?

"I can't believe I was conned by the pair of you. Are you going to tell me next that my dearly beloved late wife has a sprawling family tucked away somewhere?"

"No family, Angelo. She lived with Annie, her grandmother. I'm sorry I never mentioned my dad to you," she was constrained to tell him. "I didn't think it was important."

"Correction. You didn't want me to be influenced by it."

"Well, maybe I didn't!" Rosie burst out with sudden anger. "And can you blame me? The way you're looking at me now…!"

"Do you really think I would have given a damn where you came from?" He didn't want to become embroiled in a fruitless discussion with a woman who dug herself deeper and deeper into a hole with every sentence that passed her lips but, like a thorn, she had burrowed under his skin. "I despise liars," he imparted grimly. He wanted to ask her

what other lies might he expect from her and had to remind himself that she was no longer his concern. She was
disposable. Were it not for extraordinary and unforesee-
able circumstances, he wouldn't even be sitting here in this
cottage with her, having this conversation.

"So do I," Rosie said quietly. Did he think that she didn't
know about the way he had strung her along? Did he really imagine that he was as unblemished as pure snow?

"What is that supposed to mean?"

"Nothing," Rosie muttered. "It's just exhausting arguing with you. It's not my fault Mandy left me this cottage,
and it's not my fault that I'm grateful that she did and that
I want to live in it. I just don't accept that you have to treat
me like dirt because you happen to disapprove."

"Why did you decide to up sticks and come to London?
Why didn't you stay put and try and do something nearer
to where you grew up?"

"Sorry?" Rosie blustered. She looked at him narrowly,
searching his face for more cold, biting dislike and was
disconcerted to find none there. There might not have been
any warmth but for the moment at least his icy contempt
was not in evidence.

"Call me a masochist," Angelo drawled, "But I'm curious to discover what makes you tick."

"Why?"

"When I so completely fail to read a person, I like to
work out where I went wrong." He shrugged his broad
shoulders.

"You mean so that you don't make the same mistake
twice?"

"You're a one-off, never-to-be-forgotten learning
curve," Angelo said with a cutting lack of emotion. "Believe me, I won't be repeating the mistakes I made with
you, but I'm still curious." And he was, because her per-

sonality now seemed to fall in place. Her vigour, her stubborn refusal to conform to what other people demanded, her ability to challenge him without fear of consequences. "Where exactly did you grow up?"

Rosie sighed. If he wanted the full low-down on her background, then she would give it to him. It would be cathartic. In fact, it might even help her get over him. Every time she made the mistake of calling up that image of him in her head, which still seemed to happen with alarming regularity, she would picture him turning away from her in disgust at the person he now knew she was—someone so out of his league that it was laughable. "On a very rough council estate," she told him, daring him to snigger.

"Yet you managed to get out."

"If you don't get out when you're young, then you never get out. Have I managed to satisfy your curiosity? Because I'm beginning to feel a little tired. It's been a long day. I just want to go to bed now, get some rest." She stretched, stifled a yawn and watched him sideways as he rose to his feet and prowled for a few seconds around the room.

"It's all very bland, isn't it?" he mused. "No pictures, no photos." He turned to look at her. "Amanda could have done this up however she wanted, and yet she chose to do as little as possible with the decor once the renovations had been completed. Why do you think that is?"

"I wouldn't know," Rosie returned neutrally.

"And will you be overhauling the place once you move in?"

"I probably won't have the money," Rosie said bluntly.

"You came to London to make your fortune. Now you can't wait to leave, even though you'll end up jobless here, trying to make ends meet. What are you running away from?"

"I'm not running away from anyone!" Rosie answered

a little too quickly, and Angelo raised his eyebrows in a question.

"I don't believe I suggested that you were running away from a *person,* did I?"

Flustered, Rosie glared at him. What was he playing at? Was he trying to find chinks in her armour so that he could exploit them at a later date? How had the man she had fallen head over heels in love with morphed into this cold stranger? Scratch that, she told herself angrily. She knew how and, furthermore, if she had been his learning curve, then he had certainly been *hers!*

"Because it *is* a man you're running away from, isn't it?" he continued silkily.

Lost in her own thoughts and wrong-footed by the way he had zoomed straight in to form the right diagnosis behind her eagerness to leave London—scoring a direct hit, in fact—Rosie was hardly aware of him approaching her until she realised that he was standing right in front of her. If she reached out just slightly with her hand, she would be able to touch his hard, muscled chest. He was now her enemy, yet she was suddenly overcome with such a wave of yearning that her mouth went dry and her ability to think seemed to disappear. She edged back and bumped into the wall.

"I don't know what gives you that idea," she breathed jerkily.

"Your boss, is it? Mr Helpful who has so many useful connections in this part of the world?" His veiled, brooding eyes took in everything, from the way she failed to quite meet his gaze, to the nervous way she moistened her lips with her tongue. "Except why are you running from him if he's that terrific? Have you suddenly decided that you've made a mistake? Is he married? Some poor sucker with a couple of kids and a long-suffering wife back home?"

"I am certainly *not* having an affair with Julian!" She wanted to yell at him that he had no right to jump to conclusions like that, to speculate on her private life. Except they shared a history and, even though it had ended in bitterness, she could feel it too, the way it wrapped its tentacles around them, making it hard to remain detached. Or at least, that was how it was for her.

"And I would *never* sleep with a married man. Don't you know me at *all?*"

"A question I could debate for hours." The colour had rushed to her cheeks and her full lips were parted, probably on the onset of another verbal attack. Whatever he thought he knew or didn't know about her, right at this very moment in time he was certain of one thing—she was as vibrantly alive to his presence as he was to hers. The air between them was so charged that it almost crackled, and her body was leaning towards him, even though the expression on her face told him that she was trying desperately to back off...

Never before had he felt such an all-consuming urge to take a woman to bed, to make love to her until she was speechless. He was aware that he was breathing heavily, that he couldn't drag his eyes away from her flushed face.

"Angelo." Rosie was shocked at the sound of her own voice, husky and tremulous and shamefully provocative. She raised her hand and half-closed her eyes as she felt the warmth of his chest under her fingers. She didn't know why she was doing this. There was way too much water under the bridge for them even to have a passing acquaintance. Yet her whole body seemed to reach for him of its own accord.

Her hand on him set off a series of intense flashbacks in Angelo's head. It was almost as though he had been in limbo for three years, waiting to recapture the feel of her. It shocked him.

He curled his fingers around her wrist and pulled her hand away from him. It took almost more effort than he felt himself capable of, but he did it, then he stepped back and stared down at her with a cold, shuttered expression.

"Much as I appreciate the offer, darling, I'm going to have to turn you down. I can't help but think that your sudden interest in me might just have a little too much to do with getting me onside just in case you end up needing to save your skin."

Rosie's eyes flew open and she stared back at him, aghast and mortified. She wanted the ground to open and swallow her up. When she tried to say something, nothing emerged, and she kept staring in mute silence as his mouth curled into a half-smile and he inclined his head, before he turned around and walked out of the cottage.

CHAPTER FOUR

WHICHEVER WAY SHE tried to work the figures, the maths just wasn't adding up.

Rosie groaned with frustration and shoved the lined pad away from her. She had been back for the best part of a week and it hadn't taken long for her to grudgingly acknowledge that Angelo had been spot-on when he had listed the catalogue of potential financial disasters facing her if she moved to the cottage.

She might enjoy the dream of the simple life, away from London, but how was she ever going to be able to finance it? Julian had been sympathetic when she had explained the situation and, yes, he had some contacts. But, as he had reasonably pointed out, what restaurant owner was going to hand over lists of potential customers to someone they would see as a rival?

"You'd make a brilliant caterer," he had said, sitting her down while he'd fussed over a roux that was giving him trouble. "But caterers need capital. Special equipment for a start, depending on how many people you plan on catering for. Then there are the health and safety checks. Of course, you could always source customers who are happy for you to cook on their premises. Failing that, I could put you in touch with one of my mates who runs a fish restaurant… though it'll be a bit of a commute, to be honest."

"I don't own a car," Rosie had said, thoroughly deflated.

"Could be a small technical hitch, in that case. Bus and cab might do it but then you'd have precious little money left over… Now, taste this roux, darling, and tell me what you think…"

Jack had offered to lend her some money but she had refused. He and Brian were saving for a deposit on a house and Lord only knew when she would be able to pay him back, whatever money he lent her.

All told, it was hopeless.

Rosie felt herself on the verge of tears. She would have to sell the cottage back to Angelo. She pictured his look of smug satisfaction as she stood before him, head lowered, admitting defeat before she had even begun. And, worse than that, she would have to face the thought of him smirking, laughing at her for having made a pass at him, a pass that had been politely declined.

How could she have been so crazy? After everything that had happened between them, how could she have flipped and allowed herself to be swept up in an atmosphere of…what, exactly? Mutual sexual attraction? Or had that been her mind playing tricks on her? And, even if she hadn't been mistaken, if he had felt some twinge of attraction then what of it? In the light of everything that had happened between them, it didn't mean anything, as amply proved by his response.

She tried not to think about it. Every time the memory of that ten-second error of judgement began surfacing, she shoved it back down and thought about something else.

Now, she strolled absentmindedly towards the window to draw the curtains and thought about the figures that weren't adding up. Taking everything into account and looking at the best possible outcome, there was still a worrying shortfall in cash. She wondered whether her bank manager would be amenable to lending her the money to kick-start a business. She was a chef, working for not very much and without a great deal of experience. Could she be called a safe bet? And, if she couldn't squeeze a loan out of her bank, she would surely need to dig into her savings to get a car. Transport to and from the cottage would be impossible otherwise. There was no nearby bus route and a bicycle would be inadequate.

All over again, she began doing the sums in her head. Through a chink in the curtain, something caught the corner of her eye and she peered through, standing to one side. At just after five, it was dark. It was her day off and, having spent it in front of her computer, her calculator and pads of paper, she had been oblivious to the day passing by, only vaguely aware of the sound of rain gusting along the pavement outside.

Now her heart picked up a pace as she stared at Ian's car. He hadn't bothered to hide the fact that he was outside her house. Not directly outside, but parked a little way down the street. He had a small red sports car and she would have recognised it a mile away because on their one and only date he had spent much of the evening boring her rigid with descriptions of it. He had then insisted later, as she had backed off in an attempt to beat a hasty retreat, that she come and inspect the car for herself. He was lounging behind the wheel. Did he know that she had seen him? Did he even know that she was in the house or was he waiting for her to come back from work—and how long had he been there?

Not knowing whether she should go out and confront him, or stay put and hope he'd get bored and drive off, Rosie nervously headed for the kitchen, mobile phone clutched in her hand.

Her fertile imagination went into overdrive, even though

she told herself that there was no point imagining the worst. She knew that she would have to do *something*. Ian had managed to get into the house once before and, frankly, it was no great achievement. The house was poorly maintained and not exactly Fort Knox. The thought of him breaking in while she was asleep sent a shiver of pure fear through her. She could call the police, but would they come? They hadn't taken her complaint seriously before. Why would they suddenly decide to now? She hadn't reported his previous break-in, choosing instead to stick her head in the sand and pretend that she could deal with the situation.

As she turned over the various possibilities in her head, the phone buzzed in her hand and she stared down at it in horror, but it wasn't Ian. It was Angelo. The relief of seeing his name pop up on the screen sent every negative thought about him flying out of her head. She forgot her moment of humiliation. She forgot how much he disliked her and how much he had betrayed her trust.

"Angelo!"

Angelo wasn't quite sure why he had called her. He had been proud of the will power it had taken to walk away from the invitation that had clearly been given to him the last time they had met, but pride had made an uncomfortable bed companion. Rosie had returned to his life and, like it or not, he couldn't seem to get her out of his head. The fact that the air between them hummed and sizzled with untapped sexual energy had been made even worse by the naked desire he had seen flare in her eyes as she had gazed up at him with her hand burning a hole through his shirt.

He had always had rigid control over his life, over his actions and over his behaviour. He had prided himself on his single-minded drive. It was what had propelled him further and further away from the life of hardship into which he had been born. And then she had entered it four years ago and he had allowed his control to slip. There was no way he intended to repeat the mistake! And yet, back she was, screwing with his head.

It enraged him to think that he had deliberately gone on a date with a sexy blonde beauty two evenings ago, a friend of a friend of a friend, and had proceeded to spend the entire time with his mind on Rosie. A follow-up date had not been arranged.

One way or another, he would have to eliminate her from his life once again. He would have to press ahead with his argument that it would be better to sell the cottage to him than to risk trying to move and set up a business that might be doomed to failure. He was a brilliant negotiator. How hard would it be to negotiate her off his land?

And so on the spur of the moment, on a Friday afternoon, he had picked up his phone and called, and the instant he heard her voice he knew that something wasn't right.

It was shaky, high-pitched. He shot out of his chair and walked to the floor-to-ceiling window that gave his office a magnificent view of London's Shard and its surroundings.

"Ever enthusiastic to hear my voice," he drawled, wondering whether he had imagined a certain amount of panic when she had answered his call and then deciding that, yes, he had imagined it. If he hadn't, then he refused to be sucked into her mood swings. "We need to talk about the boundary lines around the cottage. They were never discussed when I gave the place to Amanda. She wanted land. I have a lot. I gave her a few acres in an informal arrangement. If you insist on living there, something more accurate is going to have to be worked out by lawyers. It might prove an additional expense for you, but it's essential."

"Angelo, could you come over? I'm at home. I had the day off work. Look, I know you're probably busy…" *And only got on the phone to issue another threat, another warning of the idiocy of refusing your offer of a buy-out.* "But it's important." She knew that her voice was cracking and that she had to get it together.

"What's going on?" This time there was urgency in Angelo's voice. He didn't know what the hell was going on, or even if this was some crazy act on her part, but he was already moving to get his jacket, working out in his head the meetings he would have to cancel.

"Remember when you asked me whether I wanted the cottage because I was running away from someone?"

"Keep talking. However," he felt compelled to qualify, just in case she got it into her head that he was in any way, shape or form, malleable, "don't think you can play the sympathy or the guilt card and sucker me in to taking a soft line with you about this whole issue."

"Shut up and listen to me."

No one spoke to Angelo like that. Amongst rivals in the cut-throat world of high finance and frenetic mergers and acquisitions, he was feared. Amongst women, he was treated with adulation, awe and a fawning desire to please. It occurred to him that that had never been Rosie's preferred style. It made sense when you considered that she had grown up in the school of hard knocks, just as he had.

For a few seconds, he rushed down Memory Lane at breakneck speed, remembering the way she used to tease him with no attempt to pander to his power; the way she used to argue if she disagreed with something he might have said, the way she had laid down ground rules when they had first started going out together and he had shown up late for their first date.

"I'm listening but it'd better be good."

"I *was* running away from someone—and that someone is sitting outside my house right now and I'm…I'm a little scared."

"Scared? Explain." He found that he was moving quickly now, exiting his office, only pausing to jot a few lines on some paper while his secretary looked at him in astonishment: he was leaving the office and wouldn't be back till Monday.

"I've had some problems with him in the past," Rosie confessed shakily. She knew that she was succumbing to the illusion that she was safe with Angelo. Maybe in the good old days, but not now, yet her heightened fear and her isolation in the house worked together with those remembered feelings to produce a mix which she was powerless to resist. Just hearing his dark, deep voice on the other end of the phone was strangely calming. Or maybe it was the fact that she was talking to *someone*. Maybe talking to *anyone* would have done the trick, although deep down she wasn't convinced.

"What sort of problems? Talk to me, Rosie."

"He broke into my house a week ago," she said flatly. "It's why I was so keen to leave London. Okay?"

"When you say *sitting outside your house,* what do you mean? Sitting on the pavement outside your house?"

Rosie laughed shortly. "Ian wouldn't be caught dead sitting on a pavement. Especially not in the driving rain. It might ruin his suit. He's a lawyer earning a lot of money; a good suit means a lot to him. So do appearances and lawyers earning lots of money don't sit on pavements. No, he's in his car. A bright red sports car which makes me think that…that…"

"That he wants to be conspicuous?" Angelo had hit the basement of his offices and was striding towards his car. Normally, he would be driven home, but his driver would not be expecting an early exit from the office and Angelo was going to do the driving himself. The address would be programmed into the sat nav although he had an excellent sense of direction and would probably have been able to find her place even after only one trip there in the dark.

"I'm probably being ridiculous." Rosie tried to be level-headed and adult.

"Why didn't you call the police? Were you just going to sit there until someone happened to pick the phone up and call you?" He was suddenly weirdly angry at her. She didn't spook easily. "Forget I said that," he gritted. "Sit tight and I'll be with you in half an hour."

"There's no need..." But then why else had she chosen to confide in him? She had slipped back into old ways and she hated herself for it whilst feeling strangely relieved that he was on his way. Confused, she remained silent, clutching the phone to her ear and resisting the urge to sneak back to the window and take a little peek just to see if that red car was still there or if she had imagined the whole thing.

"You can tell me that to my face when I get there," Angelo said drily. "Out of interest, what company does the man work for?"

She told him. It was one of the bigger practices in the city. Angelo nodded to himself; he knew a few people there. He would get the full story from her later but for the moment he knew what he was going to do. It was a bit of a shame that he would have to resist the satisfying desire to knock a little sense into the guy. His hand curled around the steering wheel as he cruised out of the car park and into the predictable chaos of the city.

"I'm going to hang up now, Rosie. Don't be tempted to go outside to confront him, to take any calls if he has your number and phones or even to spy on the car. Just wait for me." He knew the roads and streets of London like the back of his hand. He quickly manoeuvred the car out of the traffic and down a small street that hooked up to a series of back roads mostly used by wily taxi drivers. His body was adrenaline-charged. He could picture her cowering somewhere. He knew that she was a hell of a lot more scared than she was trying to let on because, had she not been, she would have handled the man herself. She certainly wouldn't have confided in someone she now considered her arch-enemy.

His hand tightened on the steering wheel. He was doing nothing more or less than he would do for anyone. The fact that it was Rosie was nothing that should bother him unduly. Still, something inside him felt sick at the thought of her being terrorised. He wondered whether he should have prodded a little harder when she had been vague on the subject of running away from someone, escaping to the country. His mouth tightened. He couldn't wait to cover the distance between himself and the loser sitting in the car outside her house.

Rosie sat and wondered what Angelo was going to do. An out-and-out brawl on the pavement? No. Angelo was a billionaire businessman. Billionaire businessmen didn't do stuff like that. And yet, she could easily imagine him getting into a fight with someone. He was incredibly physical. The temptation to sneak to the window and peer outside was overwhelming, and for the first time that day the business of trying to work out how she was going to afford to live in the country was not sufficient a distraction.

One and a half cups of coffee had been consumed before she heard the buzz of the doorbell, and when she glanced at the clock it was to discover that almost forty-five minutes had gone by. Where? Thinking of Angelo? It had always been so easy to waste time thinking about Angelo.

Was she falling right back into that habit? No. Special circumstances. But she leapt to her feet and was at the front door within seconds, yanking it open to an Angelo who looked as cool as a cucumber as he lounged indolently against the doorframe.

"What happened to the chain lock?" He straightened and stood back as she pulled open the door to let him in. When she poked her head past him to where there was no longer a red car parked on the opposite side of the road, he said casually, "What possessed you to hook up with a loser like that? At any rate, he's gone and he won't be back."

Rosie didn't know which of those statements to respond to first. "What did you do?"

Angelo looked down at her questioning, relieved expression and felt a surge of extreme satisfaction. The knight in shining armour. What man wouldn't feel on top of the world at such an uplifting sensation? Helping a little old woman cross the road would have induced a similar high. Possibly. Of course, this was not a woman for whom he should be doing favours, and yet…

As he strolled into the house, already feeling claustrophobic at its size and shabbiness, he still couldn't shift the feeling of pleasant satisfaction that had settled in the pit of his stomach. He couldn't remember having felt so good in a long time. It certainly made a change from the uniformly grim bitterness that had been coursing through his system for the past three years. Would he have obtained some release from that darkness if he had just done one or two little favours for passing strangers?

"I'm sorry I dragged you out here," Rosie mumbled, following him through into the kitchen where he proceeded to sit at the poky table on a chair that appeared to be a couple of sizes too miniature for his big, powerful body. "You've come straight from work. There was really no need. Can

I get you something to drink? Tea? Coffee? It's just that you called only a few seconds after I'd spotted Ian's car..."

She was babbling. She couldn't seem to help herself. Now that he was here, the feelings of relief were replaced by that uncomfortable scary *awareness* of him, the same scary awareness that had led to her crazily reaching out to touch him. She stuck her hands behind her back and pressed herself against the kitchen sink, but she was all too conscious of those sexy, lazy eyes on her. It made her pulse race, her heart jump and scrambled her brains.

"You've already mentioned that there was no need for me to come," Angelo pointed out. "I'll have a glass of wine, if you've got some. Red."

Relieved to be able to busy herself, Rosie bustled about, fetching them both a glass of red wine. When she thought about what the outcome might have been had Angelo not called at that precise moment in time, she felt tearful, shaky and quite unlike herself. With her back to him, she took a few deep breaths to steady her nerves, before turning round to hand him his glass of wine and then dropping into the chair facing him.

"Are you all right?" Angelo asked gruffly. "I promise you, he's gone for good. How did you manage to get involved with that creep?"

In automatic defence-mode, Rosie opened her mouth to argue the point, but how could she? "A friend of a friend." She sighed, staring at the glass and fiddling with the stem. "Amy thought that it was time I got a boyfriend. All work and no play and all that, and I guess I agreed with her. I needed to get out a little more, so I agreed to meet her friend's work colleague."

Angelo frowned. He wanted to tell her that she could have any man she wanted at the snap of her fingers. Why the hell go on a blind date? Didn't she read of all those times when women got into trouble meeting men they didn't know in places they weren't familiar with? He recalled that that was the way she had met *him,* and maintained a steady silence on the subject.

"And?" he prompted, when she looked as though she had come to a grinding halt.

"And I met Ian. At first…at first, he seemed okay—chatty, you know? Interested. But halfway through the evening I began to feel a little pressured. I could see that he was pretty intense. Very intense, in fact. It wasn't going to work but he didn't share that opinion." Rosie looked up quickly at Angelo's closed expression. Like it or not, he was due an explanation. Like it or not, she remembered what it once felt like to talk to him, to be the focus of his undivided attention.

"He insisted on driving me home. He was very proud of his car, and I knew that I wasn't going to see him again, so I agreed. What harm could it do? But halfway through the trip, I realised that he wasn't going in the right direction. He said he wanted to show me where he lived, that it was a fantastic warehouse conversion in Docklands. I told him no and things got a little unpleasant. He found a quiet spot to stop the car. It was late. Well, there was a bit of a struggle, but I managed to get out in one piece.

"After that I began getting text messages from him. Phone calls. I knew there were times when he was following me but there was nothing the police could do. Then, last week, he managed to get into the house, which was really scary. That was why the cottage, coming at the time it did, was like a stroke of good luck."

She was surprised to find that she had drunk the glass of wine. She looked at Angelo but she couldn't read the expression on his face. Embarrassment flooded her all over again. He had dashed out here to help her because she had asked. She had put him in the awkward position of having little or no choice. Coming on top of her last show of recklessness, what would he be thinking of her? Might he imagine that she was trying to manipulate him into something?

He already had a low opinion of her. When he had seen her at the funeral, his first response had been one of suspicion. He would never stop thinking that she was after something. Did he now think that her plea for help was part of some plan to net him, especially when she had already made it clear that she was still attracted to him—against all odds and despite the bitterness and disillusionment that had been the legacy of how their relationship had ended?

"You haven't told me what you said to him." Rosie tried to keep her voice as neutral as possible.

"I told him that I knew the movers and shakers in his company. I told him that if he ever came near you again, or contacted you in any way, I would make sure he no longer had a job to go to. I told him that I would go further than that. I would ensure that every door was slammed in his face. In short, he was left in no doubt that if he didn't do exactly what I told him career-wise he would be buried."

"You could do that?" Two bright patches of colour appeared in her cheeks. She wanted to grin. The relief of having this slice of her life sorted was immense, and for a few seconds she stopped analysing the details.

"I could do that."

"I was worried that you might get physical…"

"Not that stupid," Angelo told her wryly. "A man like that would cower and then run crying to the nearest police station. Not that it wasn't tempting. At any rate, your ordeal is now at an end. I wouldn't be surprised if the man upped sticks and disappeared to another part of the country. In fact, it wouldn't take much for me to pull a few strings and turn that into actuality."

"As long as I never have to see him again."

"There's no chance of that happening. Have you eaten?"

Rosie looked at him in surprise and then remembered that he had wanted to talk to her about boundary lines, about the wretched cottage. It brought her back down to earth.

"No, but…"

"Get dressed. You need dinner. I need dinner." He shrugged.

"Plus you want to talk to me about the land around the cottage," Rosie suggested absently.

Angelo had forgotten about that when it should have been at the forefront of his thoughts. He frowned. He didn't want to get sucked into her personal dramas. This would be the exception, because this was a drama that could have been harmful to her, and at the end of the day he wouldn't wish physical harm on his worst enemy.

"Right."

"Okay; if you give me five minutes, I'll get dressed."

Rosie was speedy when it came to getting ready. She barely wore make-up. Her wardrobe was limited, so there was little opportunity for her to stand in front of it for hours, agonising over a choice of clothing. When she had been dating Angelo, she had accumulated loads of clothes because they had gone to loads of fancy places. In the wake of their break-up she had given the lot away, and working behind the scenes in a bustling kitchen didn't require much imagination when it came to a dress code: jeans and comfortable clothes. Flat shoes.

However, she found herself dithering. She wasn't going on a date! Yet she told herself that that was no reason to look drab. What was wrong in throwing on a little make-up? And wasn't it about time she took those shoes with heels out for an airing? And that black dress? She couldn't remember the last time she had flung it on. And besides, she argued with herself, how often did she actually get to eat out? It was ironic, considering she worked in a restaurant.

When she next looked at her reflection, she was alarmed at the warm flush in her cheeks and the dress…the heels… Too late to think about changing. She grabbed a scarf to tone down the plunging neckline of the dress and hurried out of the bedroom to find Angelo waiting for her in the lounge, inspecting all the little bits she had gathered over time and which she had interspersed in the room to try and camouflage its drabness: posters of old movie stars; a picture of her smiling when she had graduated from her catering course; various vases she had picked up in boot sales and which she had arranged on the book shelf along with her selection of books, not that she ever seemed to have much time to do any reading.

"I'm ready." In the act of putting on her black coat, she missed the look in his eyes as he took her in.

Why kid himself that this rescue mission didn't have a powerful personal edge to it? Angelo thought. Looking at her now, he could feel his whole body stirring into heated arousal. The dress showed every inch of her body; hugged her small, rounded breasts, even though she was wearing a fairly hideous scarf in a vain attempt to conceal them. Like it or not, he was on a high, because the damsel in distress was *Rosie.* Clearly his body hadn't eliminated the memory of her, even though his mind surely had.

"I expect you know all the restaurants around here?" He began moving towards the door, putting on his jacket as he walked towards her.

She laughed and Angelo inhaled sharply as once again he reacted to the infectious sound. "You'd be surprised.

I never eat out. For a start, I can't afford to go anywhere nice, and then I'm working all the time."

"Hence why you felt compelled to go on a blind date with that creep?"

"I didn't know he was a creep when I went. There's supposed to be a very good Italian about ten minutes away." Having dressed up, she squashed the moment of deflation when he failed to comment. Why would he?

There was no reason to feel all fluttery and girlish, yet she did. It was a relief to be out of the close confines of his car and in the busy warmth of the restaurant which, as it was still quite early, was relatively empty.

"Thank you for this," Rosie said brightly once they were seated and menus had been placed in front of them with all the usual attendant Italian flamboyance. "I expect you must be really annoyed at having to spend a Friday evening like this—dragged away from your work to deal with problems that have nothing to do with you."

"If this is leading up to another gratitude speech, then skip it, Rosie. I'm not a hero for dealing with the wimp who was pestering you." Except it was more than just pestering and Angelo wouldn't allow his mind to go there.

"Okay." Her bright smile faltered. "Well, you said on the phone that you wanted to talk about boundaries?" She sat back to allow some wine to be poured for them and waited as their orders were taken. She could feel Angelo's eyes on her and she knew that she had to maintain a bland, cheerful front which would make things so much easier.

"It's a bit messy."

Rosie sighed and leant back in the chair. All the energy seemed to rush out of her in a whoosh.

"Before all of this, I was at home trying to do the sums, Angelo." She half-closed her eyes and folded her arms tightly around her. Then she leant forwards slightly and looked at him before dropping her eyes to the checked table cloth. "None of it works out," she said bluntly. "My boss can't really help me. I would have to go through a million hoops before I could really start to get anything off the ground. I hadn't really stopped and considered all the fine details. I was so desperate to get away from London."

Angelo flushed darkly as he remembered his option of getting some sort of revenge by allowing her to fail. He didn't say anything but he noticed, as food was placed in front of them, that she seemed to have no appetite.

For a while, she gave him the basics of why she would never be able to make a go of any catering business. It was nothing he hadn't previously pointed out to her, yet it didn't give him the expected kick of satisfaction. His mind kept coming back to the creep who had stalked her. The woman he had been happy to dismiss at the funeral as history—and bad history at that—was now doing all sorts of things to his equilibrium. Or maybe she had *never* stopped doing things to his equilibrium? He impatiently shoved that notion aside.

"I thought about going to see my bank manager," Rosie was now saying, having exhausted the topic of all the things that would be required for her to launch her own catering business. She suspected that she was boring him to death, because he wasn't saying a word. She felt that any minute now he would surreptitiously glance at his watch. Lord knew, he probably had things to do on a Friday evening. He wasn't a man who enjoyed staying in and chilling on his own.

What had his Friday evenings been like with Amanda? Her curiosity on the subject of his marriage was so huge that she knew she dare not allow it to get a foothold. She needed to keep her distance.

"But I don't think there would be any point," she perse-

vered into the silence. "I don't think I'm the most credit-
worthy person in the world." Looking down, Rosie realised
that she had barely touched the food on her plate and she
now made a few half-hearted attempts to eat a bit more. Her
nerves were all over the place. She was so conscious of him
sitting in the chair opposite her that she had to stop herself
from choking on the food. She had removed the scarf and
draped it over the back of the chair and she realised that
the shadow of her cleavage was on show. Very quickly, she
straightened up and pushed the plate slightly to one side.

"Plus I would need money for a car. Not that it wouldn't
be nice having a car," she said wistfully. "Driving lessons
were the one thing my dad set aside money for. He paid it
direct into an account which he couldn't touch because he
knew how tempted he would be on a bad day to take it all
out. He used to tell me that there was nothing like being
behind the wheel of a car."

"You should have told me about your father," Angelo
said abruptly.

Rosie wondered whether it would have made any difference. He would still have disappeared with her best
friend. That thought grounded her. "That's not relevant
now," she said with a cool shrug of her shoulders. She refused coffee and told him that it was time she was heading back to the house.

"What I think you *will* find relevant," she said, meeting his inscrutable green eyes without flinching, "Is the
decision I've reached."

"Don't keep me in suspense."

"Having tried to work out how I could afford to move to
the cottage and come up against a brick wall, Angelo, you
win. I won't move. I can't afford to. I can't throw money
I don't have after a dream and there's no need really now
anyway. I don't have to run away. So, I'm happy to sell the

cottage to you, and I don't really care how much you give me for it. I realise it shouldn't have been mine anyway. You can buy it and develop the land into whatever you want and it'll be as though we'd never met each other again."

CHAPTER FIVE

HE HAD GOT precisely what he wanted. From the very first second he had learnt that the cottage had been willed to her, Angelo had been determined to make sure that he got it back, one way or another. His preferred route would have been to haul her through the courts and watch as a legacy to which she had no right crumbled and fell apart in front of her greedy little eyes. But the will had been watertight, so he had tried to buy her out. In return, she had dug her heels in.

His one goal, his only goal, had been to remove the cottage from her, get her out of his life.

When, he wondered uneasily, had that changed? When had he discovered that she was on his mind and not all of his thoughts were charged with anger and frustration?

"Aren't you going to say anything?" Rosie pressed, annoyed now that she had been the only one talking for the past ten minutes. The bill came and went and they got up to leave, amid a flurry of exuberant gratitude from the proprietor that they had chosen to patronise his little restaurant. Even without trying, Angelo was managing to elicit the sort of fawning behaviour to which he was accustomed. When the owner expressed the wish that they come again to sample different dishes, she fought the temptation to tell him that that wouldn't be happening any time soon.

"I'll talk when we're back at your house," Angelo informed her. Frustrating though it was to admit it, he was having a hard time relinquishing the idea that she would disappear from his life as fast as she had re-entered it. He knew that he could throw a derisory amount of money at her for the cottage and she would accept it. She might be a gold-digger who had flogged the presents he had given her but she was also smart.

So, now that he could get rid of her, and everything sensible, logical and cool-headed was telling him that that was the right road to go down, why was he restlessly dissatisfied with the promised outcome?

Sex.

The word lodged in his brain, an instant answer to the questions that had popped up like nasty insects released from Pandora's Box. There was no need to look further to find the reason behind his recent distracted behaviour.

In the aftermath of their relationship, he had never quite managed to stifle the fact that he still wanted her. He had wanted her the second he had seen her in that bar. He had carried on wanting her the whole time they were together, which had been nothing short of a miracle, because longevity had never featured in any of his previous relationships. His purpose was to work, to achieve the security only wealth could bring as far as he was concerned, and women, pleasant distractions that they were, always made short-lived appearances in his frenetically busy and high-pressured life. Before Rosie his relationships had been of the hit-and-run variety and he had liked it that way.

But she had come along and, he could now admit to himself, he had never stopped wanting her even though he had ended up married to Amanda through circumstances that hardly bore thinking about.

Angelo understood the power of sex. He had felt it when

he had seen Rosie again. He just hadn't admitted its hold. Their relationship had ended in chaos. He hadn't had time to grow tired of her. Naturally, that would have happened inevitably, but at the time of her departure he had still found her insanely attractive.

Mentally piecing together the puzzle, he was pleased to have found the solution to his restlessness and to the unsavoury fact that he couldn't envisage her disappearing from his life just yet.

If he hadn't seen an answering flame in her eyes, if she hadn't made that pass at him which had been proof positive that he still affected her the way she still affected him, then maybe he wouldn't have objected to getting rid of her. Maybe he would be listening to her ramble on about selling the cottage without getting that sickening twist in his gut.

The prospect of having his life back to a place where he wasn't having to deal with annoying thoughts about her was blessed relief and he allowed himself to relax from behind the wheel of his car.

Revenge, he decided, was not to be found watching her fail in her quest to kick-start her life. Revenge, such as it was, could easily be achieved by seducing her back between the sheets and then dumping her when he had got his fill. With everything that had gone on between them, he confidently predicted that it would be a remarkably transient situation.

How long could good sex block out the fact that he didn't like her? How long before his body caught up to his brain? A week or two? And then he would be able to wash his hands of her for ever. His unfinished business would draw to its conclusion and he would be able to walk away without a backward glance. A bonus would be to have her plead with him to stay but, even if her pride got in her way and there was no such bonus, sleeping with her would be a job well done because it would obliterate the demons inside him.

He allowed himself a half-smile in the darkness of the car and he was still smiling when he pulled up in front of her house.

Forget about the running away from a stalker situation, Angelo felt that *he* would have wanted to run away if he had been stuck living in a dump such as the one he was now looking at. He wondered how often she had cursed herself over the years for not having played her cards right, for not having used all that money to do something sensible. He had no idea where it had gone and could not care less, but it certainly hadn't gone towards a deposit on a house.

"There's no need for you to come in." Rosie began unbuckling her seat belt, half-turning to glance at him over her shoulder. "You've already done enough and I can't begin to thank you." Buckle undone, she paused and sat very still, gazing down at her lap before turning to him. He was staring at her, his eyes silver in the shadowy light. She felt a tingle run through her. Time to wrap up the thank-you speech before her body went into overdrive and she did something stupid again—like try to kiss him one last time before they parted company for good. The thought of being that weak terrified her.

"Now that you've taken care of Ian, I can't believe how light I feel, as though a great big weight's been taken off my shoulders."

"Was that loser the only reason you wanted the cottage?" Angelo inserted mildly, because he was sick of being thanked for something he had taken a perverse delight in doing. Besides, without this unexpected situation, would he be here now? Ian might be a creepy stalker but he was also a pivotal player in Angelo's move forward. Because of him, Rosie had found herself in a vulnerable place and he, Angelo, had been the one to rescue her from it. Instantly the dynamics of their relationship had been subtly altered.

"Well…" Rosie looked at him, sprawled against the car door so that he could have the best possible vantage point as he lazily stared at her. "Of course, I know you thought it was all wrong that Mandy did what she did. Left me something you considered yours, and maybe she was…"

"We're not debating the rights or wrongs about what Amanda did."

"No. In that case, if I'm being perfectly honest, I guess it would have been nice to get out of London. I've been here a while and it's very hectic."

"And unrewarding too, I should imagine."

"How do you mean?" Rosie asked tentatively. It was disconcerting being here, talking to him without bitterness and anger underlying every word, but he *had* dealt with the threat of Ian and he had done so in a pretty conclusive manner, in a way no one else would have been able to—probably not even the police if they had cared to get involved.

Angelo shrugged, as though the answer was self-evident, but he would be kind enough to point it out. "Renting a place like this, throwing money down the drain—or maybe I should say straight into the hands of a landlord who probably gets by doing the minimum. Working all the hours God made in an averagely paid job which you can't chuck in because you need the experience. I guess it must be daunting staring your future in the face and maybe wondering whether this is as good as it gets."

Rosie had not considered her prospects in such stark terms. "That's not exactly fair," she protested weakly.

"But, of course, you'll have the money from the cottage to invest in something."

"I guess so."

"Although, in fairness, I suppose the competition in London must be stiff when it comes to the catering business. In fact, I have an excellent personal chef, as you know, who also has his own catering business as a sideline. I gather his most valuable clients, though, are the people who use him on a regular basis. Like me. Go on the Internet, key in 'caterers in London' and apparently you're instantly besieged with results." He sat forward, surprising her, and his arm brushed past her to open her car door before she could let loose a protest. "I'll walk you in. And please don't tell me that there's no need."

She was very much aware of him behind her as she unlocked the front door, standing so close that she could feel the warmth radiating from his body.

"Well, now that everything's been decided, shall I get Mr Foreman to contact you about the sale of the cottage? I'm not sure what happens next. Do estate agents have to get involved or can we just handle the whole thing ourselves?" Somehow he had managed to enter the house and she pushed the door slightly, leaving it ajar, a pointed hint that he was literally seeing her into the house and not hanging around for an extended social visit. He shut it firmly with his hand and stood back.

"I think after all I've been through, I deserve a cup of coffee," he murmured.

Rosie dithered but eventually acquiesced. Somehow having coffee with him here, in her house, sitting in her cramped kitchen, felt a lot more intimate than a cappuccino in a restaurant surrounded by noisy people and obsequious waiting staff.

"Have you thought how you would launch yourself into the catering business?" Once in the kitchen, Angelo pursued the topic with tenacity. If she took the money and ran, it would be the last he would ever see of her. There would be no reason for him to involve himself in her life and, having reached the conclusion that the only way he could terminate her reach into his everyday life, the only way he could get her out of his system once and for all, would be to sleep with her, he intended to steer her in the right direction.

"I only thought about it in connection with the cottage," Rosie confessed. She wished he wouldn't dwell on the venture, which seemed laden with possible pitfalls, but on the other hand wasn't it good to have someone point out those pitfalls? No one ever built a successful business with their head in the clouds, and Angelo was nothing if not the epitome of the successful businessman. Having rescued her from Ian, he was probably feeling charitable towards her, basking in the glow of a good deed done. It wouldn't last, but while the streak was in evidence wouldn't it be a good idea to pick his brains? She might know a great deal about cooking, but when it came to finance she was hopeless.

She made him a cup of coffee and, when she would have slid it across the table to him, she saw that he was standing up, heading towards the lounge.

"The lumpy sofa is slightly less uncomfortable than the rock-hard kitchen chairs," he said by way of explanation. "In case you hadn't noticed, a man of my size isn't built for chairs that small."

Rosie, who had noticed all too well, didn't comment. She followed him into the lounge where he proceeded to make himself at home on the sofa, tossing aside the bright cushions which she had bought specifically to camouflage the dreary brown covering, and dragging a coffee table next to him on which he indicated that she should deposit the cup.

"You were going to give me your business plan?" he encouraged. "You'll need one. Whatever you get from the sale of the cottage won't cover launching a new career *and* buying a house."

Rosie frowned. She had dropped into the chair furthest away from him, a rigid, hard-backed chair which obviously belonged to a dining table but had been surplus to requirements, hence had found its way into the house where it had been plonked in the lounge to fill space. It was uncomfortable, to be avoided at all costs, but where else was she to sit when he had monopolised the sofa?

"What do you mean?" She felt and sounded like a fool.

"The cottage is charming and it's in a lovely location, but it's small, and there's a limit to what you would be able to get for it. There's always a financial glass ceiling for a place like that. It also shares access to my house and most people would find that unacceptable. Also, until this situation with the boundary lines is sorted out, it can't be sold."

"Right." That hadn't occurred to her.

"I have no idea how long it will take to sort that little matter out. It could be days or weeks or months."

"I suppose it was too good to be true." Rosie sighed. "I bet you're really happy about all of this," she continued without any rancour. "Funny thing is, I felt at home there, even though I shouldn't have. It was as if I'd met the old Amanda, the one I knew before…everything." She cleared her throat and fidgeted on the chair. "One good thing is that Ian will no longer be around. I can get on with my life. I don't have to keep looking over my shoulder. There's no point doing a business plan. If and when the cottage ever gets sold, then maybe I'll think about it again. If not, then that's okay."

"You look uncomfortable on that chair." Angelo made a space for her on the sofa and patted it.

"I'm fine here." Did he feel sorry for her, the way the victor feels sorry for the person they've just vanquished?

She watched him warily as he continued to look at her, his head tilted to one side. When he stood up and strolled towards her she practically leapt out of the chair in dismay. He leant over her, hands clasping the arms of the chair on either side. She pressed herself back as far as she could go. What was he doing? He had rolled up the sleeves of his shirt and, as her eyes skittered away from his face, they were drawn to his sinewy forearms, sprinkled with dark hair.

Fascinated, she stared at the way the whorls of hair curled round the dull matt silver of his watch strap. In her mind's eye, she could remember him removing that watch, his eyes pinned to her face as he stripped in front of her. He had always been magnificently self-confident when it came to his body. More than that: he had liked her looking at him. He had once told her that there was no greater turn-on for him. She blinked but the image refused to go away because he was still looming over her.

"What are you doing?" She cleared her throat.

"Slight change of topic here."

"I beg your pardon?" Thoroughly confused, she raised her eyes to his and her lips parted. It was as though her whole body was being held in a state of suspension. She could barely breathe.

"Let's drop the subject of the cottage and whether or not it'll be sold. There's really only so much that can be said on the matter and then we're just going round in circles, repeating ourselves. No, what I'd really like to talk to you about, what's been on my mind for the past few days, is what happened the other night."

"The other night?" Rosie parroted faintly.

Angelo straightened and strolled towards the window in a leisurely manner. The old-fashioned bay window, its paint peeling, overlooked the road and was the only attractive feature in the room. He leant against it and shoved his hands in his pockets. Rosie's eyes dipped to the way the fine, expensive fabric was pulled taut over his pelvis and she looked away quickly.

"The cottage? Just before I left?"

"I'd rather not talk about that."

"Why not? I realise you might feel a little embarrassed because you made a pass at me and I turned you down, but I still think we should revisit what happened."

"I know you're bitter towards me, Angelo, but if this is your idea of fun at my expense then I'm not laughing. I said I don't want to talk about what happened and I don't. Okay, so I'm grateful for the way you handled Ian, but that doesn't mean that you can say whatever you want and humiliate me however you please. This is *my* house and I think it's time you left."

"You think that's what I'm trying to do—by talking about what happened between us."

"Nothing happened between us."

"But something very nearly did."

"It's time for you to leave."

"Are you *that* scared? You'd rather chuck me out of your house than have a conversation with me?"

"There's nothing to talk about, Angelo. I made a mistake. It was stupid of me. I can't take it back but I don't have to discuss it for your amusement."

"So maybe *I* made a mistake as well." Angelo's voice was curiously soft. It wasn't what Rosie had been expecting him to say and she looked at him with mutinous hostility. "Maybe I should have just faced reality."

"I don't know what you're talking about."

"No, you don't *want* to know what I'm talking about, Rosie. You want to pretend that you can walk away now that the business with the cottage is at a stalemate and never look back. You give instructions to a lawyer, he handles everything for you when and if you need him. But you give the game away every time you get too close to me."

Rosie stared at Angelo in terrified silence. She could keep arguing with him, telling him that he didn't know what he was talking about, except how could she deny that very obvious pass? How could she deny the way the colour bloomed in her cheeks whenever he was near, or the way her words emerged, high and unnatural? It didn't make any difference knowing that she should be distant and remote towards him. She would never forget the way he had ended things with her, the fact that he had jumped into bed with her friend and then married her. Yet on some horrible, primitive, elemental level, she just couldn't shake the effect he still had on her.

"I don't even like you," she protested weakly. "You married my best friend!" Tears gathered at the back of her throat, thickening her voice, and she looked away abruptly because she didn't want to go there. She didn't want to rake up the past. She just wanted to move on from it, except how was she going to do that when he was standing metres away from her, forcing her to face up to stuff she didn't want to acknowledge?

"And you think I had a choice?" Angelo rasped, pushing himself away from the window. He raked his fingers through his hair and grimly wondered how far he was prepared to go to get her into bed with him. Would he be prepared to unearth things that were better left buried? Would his intense pride even allow him to do that? No!

Rosie was shocked rigid by Angelo's response. She had no idea what he was talking about. Of course, he would have had a choice. There was no way that Angelo, of all people, would ever have allowed himself to be pushed into doing something he didn't want to do. And yet there had been an underlying savagery and bitterness in his denial that confused her.

"What on earth do you mean?"

"I mean we still turn each other on, Rosie. Cute, don't you think? After everything we've been through? When I saw you at that funeral… I can't believe I'd forgotten just how sexy you were. Or maybe I hadn't. Maybe I'd shoved the memory somewhere to the back of my brain, tidied it away so that it was out of sight. Is that what you did as well?"

"What did you mean when you said that you *had no choice?*"

"Let's move on from that, Rosie. I have no intention of getting mired in semantics. The past is over and done with, but unfortunately it's left us with a somewhat uncomfortable present. I turned you down the first time you made a pass at me in the cottage because I stupidly failed to think this whole attraction situation through."

Rosie was in a daze. How could he be talking about something as intense as the chemistry that still sizzled between them in a voice that was as cool and as casual as a stranger's voice? When he spoke about this whole attraction situation, he could have been discussing a curious weather system or a nasty traffic incident on the M25.

"And now?" She couldn't escape the sudden electric tension in the room.

"You look as stiff as a plank of wood," Angelo said drily. In fact, there was a part of him that was stunned at what he was doing. He was pursuing a woman who had no place in his life. He was elevating sex to something he couldn't do without. It was a weakness he felt he couldn't control, although it certainly helped dealing with it the way he was now.

"How can you expect me to be relaxed?" Rosie sprang

out of the chair and began pacing the room, her arms tightly clasped around her body. When she had impulsively taken Angelo's call and done the unthinkable, the unexpected… asked him to *help* her…she hadn't envisaged that this was where the evening would end. She stopped and looked at him from across the width of the room. "This is the most bizarre conversation I've ever had!"

"Why? Because we're talking about sex? Finishing a conversation you began when you touched me?"

"I don't know what I was thinking when I did that."

"You weren't."

"Weren't *what*?"

"You weren't thinking. You were acting purely on impulse. *I* was the one thinking and it has to be said that sometimes it pays not to think too much. Can cloud the water." Except this was a much better outcome.

"I have a proposition for you," Angelo continued as he sauntered towards the sofa, eyed it as though it might harbour infectious germs and decided against it to try the third chair in the room which, although not as challenging as the one to which Rosie had now returned, didn't offer much hope of relaxation. He might not have grown up with creature comforts but he had certainly grown accustomed to them.

"What sort of proposition?" Rosie asked warily. Her back ached from the chair but her legs were shaky, and pacing the small room like a caged bear made her feel awkward and vulnerable. The palms of her hands were clammy with perspiration and the black dress felt scratchy and uncomfortable.

Angelo leant forwards and rested his forearms on his thighs so that his hands dangled loosely between his legs. "We could go round in circles," he murmured, "sniffing each other and then backing off, but we can't hide the fact that we're attracted to one another."

"We don't like each other."

"Not the point. Over the past three years, tell me honestly, did you manage to put me out of your mind?"

Rosie thought about that blind date with Ian, the reasons that had prompted her to go on it in the first place. Since Angelo had disappeared from her life, she had hidden behind her work and entombed herself behind a wall of ice. She reddened and remained silent, which was answer in itself.

"I'm getting the picture."

"No, I don't think you are, Angelo. You think that because we happen to be attracted to one another, that we should do something about it?" There was a hysterical edge to her laughter but when she caught his eye it was to find that he wasn't sharing in the mirth.

"We don't do something about it," Angelo said coolly, "And we don't get past it."

"Of course we do. Physical attraction doesn't last. That's the whole thing about lust. It goes away, given enough time." She smoothed restless hands along her thighs. "You slept with my friend."

"Don't go there." Angelo stared her down. If only she knew the circumstances of that one fateful night, when he had been bombarded with the information that would signal the death of their relationship.

It was a memory he kept firmly locked away and he would never bring it out of hiding. It was a moment in time of which he was deeply ashamed. Drunk, wild with rage and pain. God, had he *cried?* He might have. He thought he had. How could one woman have so thoroughly burrowed under his skin? Where had his natural aptitude for self-preservation gone? Had he been so thick that he had needed someone to come along and show him the proof of his own stupidity? He had barely been aware of Amanda in the bedroom although he had certainly been stripped and far more, as it turned out, the consequences of which he could never have envisaged.

"You're crazy."

"Am I?" He stood up with lazy intent and she was frozen to the spot as he walked slowly towards her. When he was standing in front of her, he reached down and trailed one long, brown finger against her cheek.

In her head, Rosie was pretty sure she was objecting to that fleeting, horribly intimate caress. Barely a caress. Just a feathery touch. Unfortunately, her head had stopped communicating with her body which had been galvanised into shamefully instant response. Wetness spread between her legs, dampening her underwear. She could feel it. And then, galloping away at a tangent with breakneck speed, a series of graphic images leapt into her head: thoughts of that lazy finger stroking between her thighs, parting the soft folds that protected her clitoris, rubbing the small bud until she was crying out for more. Her breasts felt heavy, the nipples tight and sensitive. He knew her body so well. It was as though no time at all had elapsed since they had been lovers.

How was this possible? How could she be feeling like this? But she knew that it was the same violent physical reaction, as instinctive as a knee-jerk, that had driven her to reach out and touch him at the cottage.

He nudged his thigh between her legs, pushing it up and under the stretchy dress, and moved his knee with gentle but demanding pressure so that waves of sudden pleasure made her gasp aloud. No one had touched her since him. She hadn't even been able to conceive of letting anyone

near her. Having him touch her now electrified her body
and her eyelids fluttered.

"You're hot for me." Angelo was holding on to his self-
control by a thread. "I can feel it… I can *hear* it…"

"Angelo, please."

"Please *what?* Please bring me to orgasm? Or maybe
please put your mouth where your knee is? Because I know
how much you like that, Rosie, just like I know how sensitive your nipples are, how one lick of my tongue can almost make you come."

He reluctantly removed his legs where a damp patch at
the knee was proof of how turned on she was by him, despite the fact that she had mouthed all the right words and
made all the right objections.

He knelt down next to her so that they were eye-level.
Rosie was still breathing quickly, panting almost. She wriggled up into a sitting position and pulled her dress back
down because it had been pushed up over her hips. Her
hands were shaking. She could barely think straight. She
felt shell-shocked.

"I have yet to tell you my proposition," he murmured
and tilted her face to his when she would have looked away.

"I know what it is, Angelo. We fall into bed like a couple of horny teenagers who are too stupid to think through
the consequences."

"You want to go into catering? I will set you up with
your first big job. In Cornwall. I know everybody who's
anybody down there and the rest would jump at a chance
to nose around the manor. You won't need to invest in any
equipment. I'll even throw in a small car. You can pay me
back when you start making money or if the cottage is
sold." He shrugged. "Or you can not pay me back at all.
It's immaterial…"

Rosie blinked. Never had such soothingly spoken words

carried such dangerous intent. She was listening to him propose a pact with the devil. Her mouth parted and she made an inarticulate, strangled sound under her breath.

"I know. Thrilling, isn't it? Just when you thought your ship had sunk."

"I can't believe I'm hearing this."

"Don't bother trying to work a maidenly exit, Rosie. You'll never be able to pull it off. I'm offering you the deal of a lifetime, so to speak."

"I'm not a…a…"

"I think I know the word you're striving to say, but let's leave that unspoken. I like to think that what we have here is the perfect arrangement." He idly traced the contour of her breast and then laughed when she primly pulled away. "Horse, bolting and locking the stable door springs to mind."

He stood up, pulled the chair over so that they were facing one another and he leant back to hook his arms over the back.

"How can you even begin to tell me that sleeping together is *the perfect arrangement?*"

"Let's not forget the perks: happiness, prosperity and moving on lie just round the corner. And, just to throw a little more sweetener into the deal, you move into the cottage, we have our fling, wean ourselves off one another and I sell up when it's all over and done with." He allowed the thought to take shape and form: *at least when I decide it's all over and done with…*

"You *sell up?*"

"I can't see the pull of owning a place when you live on the grounds. Whether you own some of the land or not is a technicality. I imagine we'll be only too glad to be rid of one another when our time's up."

"But I thought you wanted to develop the grounds."

"Into a luxury hotel complex but, quite honestly, I'm expanding at some speed into the Far East. I could probably do without the hassle of opening something in Cornwall. The money in IT is guaranteed. The money in a hotel complex less so. Originally, it might have been a hobby of sorts, but I'm more than willing to ditch that hobby for, let's just say, the cause for the greater good." He shrugged. "At any rate, I have a chain of boutique eco-hotels across Europe. One more hotel might just fall into the category of overkill."

"How can you be so cold?"

Angelo's mouth twisted into a smile. Really? How could *he* be so cold? She was priceless. She had fleeced him and more, yet she had the brazen cheek to talk to him about *being cold*.

"So, to recap," he said. "You move into the cottage. I can't imagine you'll miss this hell-hole. If you need to lose your deposit, then you'll be compensated. I will immediately host a party or any number of parties so that your name is circulated. I have some impressive company contacts there as well. A word in the right ear will guarantee business for you.

"My boundary lines are any personal discussion of what happened in the past. We won't be in the business of post mortems; we'll be in the business of scratching an itch." He delivered a wolfish, amused smile that didn't quite manage to reach his eyes. "You think I'm cold—I'm realistic. It's been three years and you still went up in flames the second I touched you and it's the same for me. I don't want you in my head any more than I suspect you want me in yours and the only way to kill that dead is to get into bed and exhaust whatever nagging remains of passion we have left."

"And if I don't go along with that?"

"You will, Rosie. All your boxes have been ticked. You stand to gain a lot. Why wouldn't you?"

CHAPTER SIX

WHY WOULDN'T SHE? What sort of crazy question was *that?*

Because there was no way that she would sell herself? No way that she would allow herself to be touched by a man who gave away his hatred for her with every syllable that passed his lips? How could he offer an arrangement of sex without any involvement, without any conversation? How could he think that they could climb into bed and forget everything that had happened between them, pretend that none of it had ever existed?

Rosie wished she had been as coherent then as she was now, three days later. In fact, faced with his outrageous suggestion, she had barely managed to stutter a half-baked, lame and uncertain protest before being left gaping like a stranded gold fish as Angelo had let himself out, leaving her to ponder his proposal.

It was all well and good being clever post-event. Being able to formulate some very articulate rebuttals to his crazy proposition in the quiet of her own house. Unfortunately, she was unable to deliver her scathing, icy speech because he had left the country for business in Singapore. In closing, his text promised that they would talk when he returned to the country.

Rosie had no intention of doing any such thing. However, she did telephone James Foreman, who indeed confirmed that selling the cottage would be a long-winded business entirely dependent on the matter of the boundary lines being sorted. Angelo had not foreseen a circumstance in which the land would have to be legally divided and so had taken no precautions.

"Well." Rosie inhaled deeply and made her mind up on the spot. "I won't be selling just at the moment." Angelo's brutal summary of her achievements thus far and the promise of a future that was barely better than the present had made her think. She could spend the rest of her days trying hard to set up her own business, fighting competitors with far more experience, possibly investing money to see it go down the pan, or she could turn her back on the bright city lights and take her chances in a much smaller pool. The potential clients might be fewer but so would the competitors.

There was no way that she intended to accept charitable handouts from Angelo in return for sex, but why shouldn't she do her own canvassing? Why shouldn't she move into the cottage, get calling cards printed and put leaflets through doors? Maybe get Jack to design a website for her? He was clever at things like that.

Why should she crawl back into the limited space she had erected for herself and not take advantage of a windfall? Amanda would never have left her the cottage unless as some expression of regret for the way things had unfolded and the part she had played in that. James Foreman had said as much and Rosie believed him.

Why should Rosie now just lie back and give up? Why should she think that the only way she might be able to make a go of things would be with Angelo pulling strings on her behalf? Why should she allow him to be the empowering hand inside the puppet?

Three months ago, Rosie would not have considered

leaving London, even though Ian was on the scene. She had always assumed that she had bought into the big-city life and there she would remain, struggling to make her way up. Amanda, the friend who had ruined her life, had also perversely now provided her with a choice that could enable her to forge another life for herself. And hadn't Angelo told her that he would sell up if she lived in the cottage? Of course, at the time, he had been foolish enough to think that the selling up would occur once they had tired of each other.

Rosie smirked when she thought about the insanity of his assumptions! She wondered whether he had thought that she would go along with what he wanted because he had rescued her from Ian. Had it been a *quid pro quo* situation?

If she moved into the cottage, the whole business of the boundary lines could be dealt with at leisure. It paid to be optimistic. If you looked for problems, you would find them, and she wouldn't let Angelo scare her away by pointing out everything that could go wrong. She wouldn't give him that power over her. Nor would she let herself be manoeuvred into a position of sleeping with him. He could be devilishly persuasive and he wouldn't hesitate to take advantage of the fact that he had done her a favour in getting rid of Ian.

She was so buoyed up by her sudden burst of optimism that she couldn't wait for Angelo to call so that she could set him straight and was unreasonably put out when he failed to get in touch.

"He probably got the message loud and clear and has decided to back off," she told Jack, two weeks later as she prepared for her final trip to the cottage, the one that would sever her ties with London.

She had made various journeys down, taking her possessions with her in stages. It had been a costly exercise, and she had had to dip into her meagre savings, but the light at the end of the tunnel was a terrific motivator. She had also had business cards printed and fliers done. Hundreds of them. She had already begun targeting various companies. Jack had done a website.

"Or maybe," Jack pointed out, "he's found someone else. After all, he's a free man now. Maybe he's decided that he's better off with someone who doesn't have anything to do with his past."

"Let's hope so." Rosie realised that that had not occurred to her. Whilst she had been busily hating him and rehearsing her contemptuous, disdainful speeches that would show him just how mistaken he had been in thinking that she might actually fall into bed with him because he wanted to tie up loose ends—while all that had been going on in her head, playing over and over like a stuck record—she actually had not considered the possibility that he had just become bored with the whole proposition and decided to shrug his shoulders and walk away.

She had not considered the possibility that she actually might not see him again. She really hadn't thought that he might have decided that pursuing a reluctant ex was more trouble than it was worth.

She chatted to Jack for a short while longer. He promised to visit once she had settled in. They spent ten minutes rehashing Angelo's dramatic success in dispatching Ian. All the time, Rosie was aware of a hollowness inside her at the thought of Angelo disappearing without a backward glance, and she told herself that it was simply frustration born from having concocted a wonderfully sarcastic speech in her head and having been denied the opportunity to deliver it.

She was *overjoyed* that Angelo had backed off. She

couldn't wait to get started on this new phase of her life and it would be a distinct advantage not having him lurking in the background, bitter and vengeful and a constant hateful reminder of a past she had struggled to put behind her.

At least, that was what she told herself over the next fortnight, during which she discovered just how inadequate her savings were as she saw them being nibbled away in the purchase of plants, essential kitchen equipment, paint so that she could brighten up some of the walls, and food. There was no money coming in. Her phone remained silent.

By week three, just as desperation was beginning to take the gloss off her upbeat mood, she received a call for her first job—but not until she had provided a comprehensive list of dishes she had cooked, the restaurant in which she had been an apprentice and her experience of cooking for crowds.

Rosie was over the moon and she was beaming when, that evening, the doorbell rang and she pulled open the door to see Angelo standing on the doorstep. She hadn't known whom to expect. She hadn't wasted a single second wondering if her visitor might be unwelcome, or even wondering who on earth could be ringing her doorbell when she had as yet to make any friends in the area. Swept away by the euphoria of having her first client, she just hadn't been thinking at all.

All over again, she was bombarded by conflicting emotions: disappointment, dismay, alarm. None of those featured even though she tried to get her mind into the place she had spent the past few weeks carefully training it to go. Instead, she felt a horrible swoop of dizzying excitement coupled with a charge of high-voltage anticipation that made her feel as though her body had suddenly been plugged into an electric socket.

"Village life seems to suit you," Angelo murmured. "Your eyes are gleaming. You look relaxed."

His absence for the past month had been intentional. He had put his cards on the table. He would back away, give her time for his proposal to sink in. Hot pursuit was not going to be his style. He had done that once and she hadn't been worth the effort, as it turned out. No, he intended to have her, and he would make sure that he was in control every step of the way.

"What are you doing here?" Rosie scrambled to get her wits together.

"Did you miss me?"

Rosie went bright red. "No. I did not miss you, Angelo. I've been busy settling in. Why are you here?"

"You've painted the walls. Why that colour blue?"

"You still haven't told me why you've come here," Rosie said bluntly. "I'm very busy."

"Doing what?" Angelo was enjoying himself. He liked the tinge of pink staining her cheeks and the furious downturn of her perfectly shaped mouth. She was wearing a pair of denim-blue overalls. One of the shoulder straps was buckled, the other wasn't, so that her cream vest, snugly outlining her breasts, was exposed. She had obviously been doing some gardening at some point during the day. The weather was lovely, with blue skies, and there was a cool, pleasant nip in the air.

"No, don't answer that," he drawled. "You've been out in the garden." He reached out to pluck a couple of dried twigs that had been caught on the thick fabric and Rosie stepped back quickly.

"Just a twig," he said, holding it up between his fingers. "Proof positive that you've been getting down and dirty with Mother Nature. It's a far cry from the girl I used to go out with."

"The girl you used to go out with worked in a cocktail bar," Rosie retorted, body still humming from where he had casually and briefly touched it.

"Aren't you going to invite me in? This seems to be the question I'm forced to ask every time I show up on your doorstep."

"That probably means that you shouldn't show up on my doorstep."

"Except you weren't complaining last time, were you, Rosie?" Angelo murmured softly, just in case she conveniently decided to forget his sterling performance as her knight in shining armour. He had done little but think about seeing her again over the past month. His powers of concentration had been lamentably creaky. Now that she was standing in front of him, he intended to use every weapon in his arsenal to get her exactly where he wanted her. He had a powerful flashback to Amanda's revelations and felt a cold, hard streak of rage and undiluted determination to get Rosie back into his bed and begin the process of clearing her out of his system.

Rosie pulled back the door and stood aside as he once again invaded her space. Her heart was beating like a jackhammer. She struggled to remember the confident way she told Jack that she was relieved that Angelo hadn't been in touch. He was as graceful and as dangerous as a panther and she couldn't tear her eyes away from him as he stood in the small flagstoned hall, rocking back slightly on the balls of his feet as he nodded approval at her choice of colour for the walls.

"I'm not going to spend the rest of my life being grateful to you because you got rid of Ian," she told him evenly.

"Eternal gratitude is something I could live without."

"But you still think that it's necessary to remind me of what you did."

"Tell me what you've been up to while I've been away." Angelo smoothly diverted the conversation. When he looked at her, he made sure to keep his eyes firmly focused on her face, yet he was taking her all in, every delectable inch of her, tallying the reality with the image that had haunted him for the past weeks. Never had he had so many cold showers.

"Mr Foreman said that the business with the land and the boundary lines could take for ever." She managed to galvanise her body into some kind of movement and walked past him, through the kitchen and out to the back of the cottage where she had begun working on the garden, dividing the fertile earth into separate plots so that she could cultivate the herbs and vegetables she knew would be useful when more catering jobs hopefully began rolling in.

Out of the corner of her eye, she watched as he sat on the deck chair she had bought cheap at one of the garden centres. He wasn't dressed for the great outdoors. His highly polished handmade shoes had already garnered some mud. His jacket looked out of place, as did his white shirt, even though he had removed his tie, probably stuffed it into his trouser pocket, a habit she was familiar with.

"What are you sniggering at?" Angelo asked, stretching out his long legs and tilting back in the chair so that the spring sun warmed his face.

"I suppose you're out of your comfort zone sitting here, aren't you? Your shoes are going to be muddy. You need to be in an office in those clothes, not out here." They had only ever enjoyed London when she had been with him, enjoyed all the sophisticated restaurants, expensive theatres and dark, intimate clubs. They hadn't taken trips out to the countryside. The memory had the fuzzy quality of a dream.

By way of response, Angelo kicked off his shoes, removed his socks, rolled up the trousers to the knees and tossed his jacket over the handle of the wheelbarrow into which a mound of weeds was steadily accumulating.

"Better?" he drawled. "Or do I need to remove some more?"

Rosie furiously dug away at the weeds and tried to ignore that sexy rhetorical question. Their unfinished conversation hung in the air between them and she didn't know what to do about it. Should she launch into the speech she had spent the past month rehearsing? Should she tell him in no uncertain terms that she wasn't up for grabs, that she didn't need him doing her any favours? That whatever attraction she felt for him was just not strong enough for her even to contemplate doing something about it?

"Your jacket will be ruined," she pointed out.

"There are plenty more where that came from."

Rosie resentfully brushed her hands clean against her dungarees, neatly folded the jacket and rested it on the other deck chair occupying the patio space.

"No need for you to do that," Angelo drawled, tilting his head to watch her as she resumed her weeding. "But then I guess old habits die hard."

"I'm disappointed that you're still a slob." She was annoyed that he was perfectly right. When they had been together, he had found her annoyance with his sloppy habits amusing. He left things lying around, told her that there was no need to pick them up, that he had a daily housekeeper who did that, and she ignored him and complained that expensive clothes should be treated properly.

Angelo laughed, relaxed. "I've never told you this, but it's one of the upsides of having made a lot of money. I don't like tidying up behind myself and I can now afford to pay someone to do it for me."

"You've always had a lot of money." Rosie sat back on her haunches and shielded her eyes against the evening sun to look at him narrowly. She knew that it was dangerous, allowing herself to enter into a dialogue with him, but she was curious. Their affair had been fast, furious and blissfully intense. It had never had time to morph into the calmer stage where questions were asked and small personal details were unearthed. It had suited her. The longer he didn't know about her past—not that she had deliberately tried to conceal it—the better. He had likewise avoided mentioning his and she had simply assumed that his wealth was far-reaching and hereditary. Who cared? It had all been peripheral to everything else: the passion, the fun, the mad, wonderful heady feeling of being on a roller-coaster ride with a guy she had fallen deeply in love with.

"My mother worked two jobs," Angelo said drily. "One of which was cleaning. My father wasn't on the scene. So, you see, maybe there's a psychological link there? Maybe having the ability to afford to pay someone to tidy up the mess I make is a permanent reminder of how far I've come?" Angelo wasn't sure why he had suddenly decided to share that with her. Hell, did it matter? Yet, sharing confidences had never been his thing. Transported from poverty in Italy to all the trappings of privilege associated with a top private school, he had learnt quickly that the less said the better.

"You never said." Rosie furiously uprooted some weeds and rocked back to inspect her handiwork but her mind was one-hundred-percent focused on Angelo. She retired to the deck chair, shifting the neatly folded jacket to the wrought-iron table, recently bought at auction for next to nothing. "When did you come over here?"

Having initiated the conversation, Angelo was now compelled to prolong it even though he really didn't want to. Chatting wasn't the purpose of his visit. He frowned at her and clicked his tongue impatiently when she continued to look at him with that disingenuous, appealing curiosity that he now knew better than to trust.

"I was thirteen." He shrugged. "I won a scholarship to come here to board. The local council had initiated a programme of trying to generate interest in education by promising to pay for the top three students in various deprived schools to study in the UK. It was a joint deal with three boarding schools."

"And you won."

Angelo grinned wryly. "My mother persuaded me that it was a good idea. I think she predicted gloom and doom and a general descent into all sorts of untold horrors if I stayed where I was. At the age of thirteen the doom and gloom prediction held a lot of appeal, but I came over and never looked back."

"Could you speak any English?"

"How much Italian did you speak when you were thirteen?"

"It must have been terrifying." It sent a weird frisson through her to think how much they had in common, had they but known it. Two people from disadvantaged backgrounds doing their best to escape, the difference being that his escape was conclusively a million times more successful than hers had been.

"Do you feel sorry for me?" Angelo murmured, injecting just the right note of cynicism in his voice to deter her from going down the "bleeding heart" road. The route from A to B didn't include tea and sympathy.

Rosie stiffened. He was very politely pointing out the chasm between them, warning her to pay attention to it just in case she got it into her silly little head to think that any conversation between them could ever be really and truly amicable. She was reminded that he hadn't come here to chat. He had come here because he had an agenda and she would have to deal with that.

"I need to go and have a shower, Angelo." She stood up and flexed her muscles which had stiffened up. "I take it you're going to be staying up at your house? Wherever that is?" How she had been tempted to have a wander and take a look but she had fought down the temptation. "So, if you haven't come here for a reason, then you should leave now."

How long, he thought, could they dance round the main event, pretending it wasn't there?

He looked at her slowly, taking his time, and when his eyes were back on her face it was to find that her colour was several shades brighter.

"I'll just sit here for a short while longer and appreciate the scenery. I'm keen to find out how you're progressing with your plans." He knew how she was progressing. In fact, thanks to him, she had just received her first order and he predicted it wouldn't be the last. Watching her fall flat on her face was no longer his objective, if it ever really had been. How receptive would she be if she was agonising over money and counting ways to avoid the poor house?

Rosie hesitated. Maybe this was the right time to tell him that she wasn't interested, that he was crazy to imagine that she would ever, ever go anywhere near a bed with him again.

In her head, she had a vivid image of a boy of thirteen, speaking no English, arriving at an exclusive boarding school with a suitcase of second-hand clothes and cheap shoes. She had known what it felt like to be stared at by upper class kids her own age. There had been one of those schools on the outskirts of the town where she had lived and the shopping mall had been the meeting ground for all teenagers, rich and poor alike. Every weekend, the boys had ogled and assumed that she would jump at the chance of nabbing one of them. The girls had smirked and looked her up and down because of her striking good looks, clutching shopping bags from stores Rosie could only dream of ever entering. Her heart went out to the kid who had had to fight his way past that to get where he was.

She had to yank herself back to the reality of the man in front of her, the man who had dumped her for her friend and now wanted to manipulate her into sleeping with him because he still happened to fancy her. As if that counted for anything.

"My plans are going really well, as it happens," she told him coolly.

"Really? I'm all ears." He stood up, reached for his folded jacket and the shoes he had earlier kicked off.

It hardly seemed fair that despite the rolled-up suit trousers, the bare feet and the shirt half-untucked from the waistband of his trousers, he still managed to look rakishly, dangerously sexy. How many men could pull off that look? Rosie wondered irritably.

"I'll follow you in," he said, gesturing for her to lead the way.

Rosie hesitated for a few seconds then packed up a few things and headed for the back door.

"Should I leave my muddy shoes out here?" he asked with such innocence that Rosie turned to glare at him. Angelo held up the shoes, the soles of which were covered in a thin layer of top soil. She had kicked hers off at the door and was now in her thick socks.

"Your house looks very clean," he expanded, "And I know you've always found my messiness a little annoying."

"Yet somehow you never bothered to change your ways," Rosie found herself retorting.

"It's not my fault that you were always such a vision

of sexiness when you were bending down to pick up my jackets."

Rosie inhaled sharply. She didn't want this. She didn't want to remember the way he would sometimes grab her, reduce her to breathless giggles as he peeled her clothes off and flung them to the four corners of whatever room they happened to be in, pretending to bribe her into making passionate love by promising to pick up all the scattered clothes himself.

"We need to talk, Angelo."

"You were going to tell me all about your move and how you've been doing with your new career."

"I know why you've come here. You want to talk about what you said the last time we met." She folded her arms and stayed her ground.

"Remind me."

"I've got my first job, Angelo. It's not enormous but it's perfect and I'm really hopeful that it's going to lead to other jobs. I'm going to make a success of this business and I'm going to give it my best shot living here in the country. I like it. It makes a great change from living in a city. It's peaceful. I don't need your help in finding work. If I succeed or fail, I'm going to do it without you, because I think it's best that we walk away from each other right now. If not for Mandy's death, we wouldn't be standing here having this conversation. We don't need to…to…"

"To what?"

"You know what I mean!" She wondered how he had somehow managed to encroach her personal space without her noticing, so that he was standing directly in front of her.

"I know exactly what you mean." He gently hooked his finger under the strap of the dungarees still on her shoulder.

"What are you doing? Don't do that!" She slapped his hand but he was smiling at her, that gorgeous crooked smile that had always been able to do all sorts of weird things to her equilibrium. When he smiled like that, all the unpleasantness was forgotten. None of it had ever existed. It was just the two of them in their beautiful, sensuous world, far, far away from reality and the rest of the human race.

She was breathing quickly. When she took a step back, she bumped against the wall. Her eyes were glued to his face, mesmerised by his eyes and that sexy half-smile. He leant against the wall next to her, crowding her so that it was hard to think straight.

"I'm glad you turned down my offer for help," Angelo said softly.

"You are?"

"I wouldn't want to put you in a position of subservience, despite what I may have implied the last time we met." Both straps were now off her shoulders so that the bib of the dungarees had flapped down. Her small breasts were pushing against the tight vest. He could make out the outline of her stretchy bra. It had always amazed him that, despite her job working as a cocktail waitress, she had had curiously prissy tastes when it came to her underwear. "I want to touch your breasts, Rosie. Will you let me? You know you want me to. We both know that."

"You don't get it. It doesn't matter." Her voice seemed to be coming from a long way off. She knew she should decisively pull the straps of her dungarees back up, but her arms hanging at her sides were as heavy and as useless as lead weights.

"If it didn't matter, I wouldn't be here and you wouldn't be trying as hard as you could to pretend that you'd be better off with me gone."

"We've already tried the whole relationship thing, Angelo!"

"Like I said, I'm not talking about a relationship. There's

no going back there for us and never will be. No, this will be much simpler, much cleaner." Talking to her was driving him crazy. He had spent weeks thinking about touching her, making love to her, looking forwards to a point when she was no longer an uninvited part of his life, gatecrashing his peace of mind and sabotaging his concentration. He didn't intend to spend days, weeks, wooing her into compliance, not when they both knew what they wanted.

He tugged the vest, which was gratifyingly slippery, pulling it up and over her breasts, breathing hoarsely and briefly closing his eyes at the sight of the little flowered stretchy scrap of cloth covering her. God, hadn't she got rid of that bra? She'd always refused to be coerced into lacy underwear and he had gradually grown accustomed to her boring stuff, grown to love each and every nondescript item. Hell, how could he even think straight when he was fixated, *captivated,* by what he was looking at?

The overalls had dipped to below her waist, exposing her slender ribcage, the perfect flatness of her belly. She carried not a spare ounce of weight on her. More than anything else, Angelo did not want to waste time remembering how easy it had been for him to lose control with her. He was in control now, even though it didn't quite feel that way. There was nothing spontaneous about this.

"Angelo."

"I've always liked it when you said my name like that, in that breathless little voice."

"We can't. There's too much history between us."

"Forget the history." He circled her waist with his big hands and moved them rhythmically upwards, stroking her ribcage until his thumbs were brushing the underside of her bra. "The only thing I want you to think about is what I'm doing to your body."

As quick as a flash, he slid his hands underneath the stretchy bra and cupped her small breasts in his hands. The bra rode up over his knuckles and he shuddered when he looked down to the perfect mounds with their big, circular pink discs. "Tell me you don't want this," he grunted, edging closer so that she could feel the steel hardness of his powerful erection.

Rosie's arguments were blurring, getting jumbled up as he began playing with her nipples, teasing the taut buds into stiff arousal.

"You hate me," she whimpered. Her body wanted to sag and, as if he knew her better than she knew herself, could read her responses and react accordingly, Angelo scooped her up to carry her upstairs, working out the location of her bedroom by instinct and kicking open the door to a freshly painted room dominated by an old brass bed.

He deposited her on the bed, stood back and began to undress.

We need to clear the air, Rosie wanted to shout. There were questions that demanded answers and explanations she needed to have, but the weight of the three-year silence between them pressed on her like a smothering hand. What was the point having long discussions? Where would it lead? Nowhere. Stripped bare, wasn't Angelo right? There was still this *something* between them that needed killing off. It was intense, it was physical and it had been lying dormant inside her ever since they had gone their separate ways. She didn't want that *something* to be her permanent companion any more than he wanted it to be his.

Stubborn pride and her sense of morality might wage war against the cold-blooded prospect of sleeping with him, but all her arguments crumbled when he was standing naked in front of her, bigger than she remembered. She wriggled out of the dungarees while he watched. His bold erection matched the slick wetness between her thighs and both were testament to how powerful the attraction between them still was.

With a sigh of hopeless resignation, Rosie surrendered to the inevitable.

"Good," Angelo breathed with satisfaction. "You've stopped trying to have a debate on the subject."

He sank onto the bed. Her bra had been discarded and her breasts pouted up at him, tantalising and provocative. But, before he really began to explore their sweetness, he pulled off her underwear, which was a little flowered G-string that matched the bra.

Her nakedness was headily familiar. The feel of her long, supple body hit him with the force of coming home and he ruthlessly squashed the bittersweet tide of memories surging up. This wasn't about the past or remembering: this was sex devoid of all emotional content or connection. He pressed his body against hers, nudging apart her legs and inserting his muscular thigh between them so that he could rub the wetness there until she was pushing back in response, building up the rhythm that had always been there the second they had fallen into bed. Their bodies had learnt how to move together, and in a heartbeat it all came back.

When he eased off, Rosie squirmed to renew the contact, but he buried her protests with a fierce, hungry kiss, their tongues melding and meshing in frantic urgency. She hadn't touched another man for three years and, released from its sexual drought, her body was quickly galvanised into heated, wanton reaction. She curled her fingers into his dark hair, drawing him to her, and then groaning with pleasure and arching back as he trailed hot kisses along her neck before descending to her breasts to take one throbbing nipple into his mouth.

The honeyed sweetness of her nipple was almost enough

to make Angelo lose control. He had to fight to restrain himself from entering her. As he licked and teased the hardened bud, nipping and suckling, he squarely planted his hand between her legs. He slid two fingers into her and, as he rubbed, she moaned and whimpered and bucked, wanting more than just that.

Her slippery wetness on his fingers was driving him wild. Anticipation of feeling that wetness embrace his hard shaft was even more of a ferocious turn-on and he was going to take his time; he was going to build up slowly to a moment he seemed to have spent all these lost years waiting for.

He withdrew his fingers to curl them around her slender waist and then he began working his way down her flat, firm belly, tasting, licking and relishing the salty tang of her perspiration. Her stomach rose and fell quickly in time to her jerky breathing. As she parted her legs wider, he groaned softly at the sight of her opening up for him, as beautiful as a flower unfurling to reveal itself.

Very gently, he flicked his tongue over and along her clitoris and felt it expand and throb as he continued to tease it. He didn't know how long he would be able to sustain an erection that was desperate for release. The musky scent of her filled his nostrils and, as he licked her, he expertly threatened sensory overload by slipping his fingers in so that there was no bit of her that wasn't responding. Her fingers were curled into his hair and, when he stole a glance up, he could see that she was poised on the tipping point, her eyelids fluttering and her beautiful mouth half-parted on a cry of intense pleasure.

"Please, Angelo."

"Not yet, baby. I want you to take me in your mouth and then, when neither of us can stand it any longer, I'll come in you. I want us both exploding at the same time."

CHAPTER SEVEN

WHEN ROSIE TRIED to compare what she and Angelo had now with what they'd had three years ago, she was at a loss. In a lot of ways, it was piercingly sweet and achingly familiar, and in many other ways it was as though she was involved with a completely different human being.

He had built an impenetrable barrier around himself and there was no way she could get past it. She had known that within days of them recommencing their relationship, if it could be called "a relationship."

Rosie gazed out of the kitchen window to where the vegetable plot she was cultivating was beginning to take shape. On the upside, the catering was doing well. That first job, nearly six weeks ago, had generated several others and she now had a girl from the village who came in to help her when needed.

On the downside…

She stared at the bowl of chopped vegetables awaiting her attention.

Her body had never been more fully satisfied. Their love-making was fast and furious and always left her completely spent. Angelo would come down on a weekend, and he would stride into the cottage with one thing and one thing only on his mind, and her body would weakly and helplessly respond. He never stayed the night. He returned to sleep at his own mansion, to which she had yet to be invited.

There was a part of her that knew just how pathetic that was, how low her self-esteem must surely be to find herself in a situation where the only thing that mattered was sex. Deep down, Rosie knew that that was the huge difference between what they had now and what they had had then. In her mind, she labelled her old relationship as "before fallout" and before fallout, she'd been a girl madly in love, where every touch was invested with significance and every kiss carried the promise of a future.

There was no future in what they had now and that was made abundantly clear in a thousand different ways. Angelo was assiduous when it came to using protection, which was a blessing, but she got the message loud and clear that very first time—her body had been screaming for him and he had calmly donned protection, whilst informing her that any mistake that could possibly lead to an unwanted pregnancy would be nothing short of catastrophic.

The past was never mentioned. Underneath the surface, she could feel the ugly swirl of unanswered questions struggling to rebel against their imposed silence.

Why had he married Amanda? Had he loved her? Had it just been the sex? What had happened to the marriage?

On the single occasion when she had tried to introduce what had happened between them three years previously into the conversation, she had watched as the passion on his face was replaced by a cold, shuttered expression that had sent a chill down her spine.

Rosie wondered how long she would be able to last. How long before she cracked under the pressure of trying to maintain the same cool, unemotional front he found so easy? Every time they made love, she was convinced that it would be the last time and she hated herself for fearing the

inevitable outcome; she hated her weakness for still wanting him so badly that it hurt, even though she always made
sure that she was as cool and as cynical as he was, treating
him with the same emotional distance as he treated her.

She heard the sound of his car pulling up on the drive.
Early summer had arrived with a bang and, although it
was already after eight, it was still bright and light outside. All the predictions she had made about the flowers
blooming into riotous colour had been fulfilled. London,
in comparison, was a grey place that was fast becoming
a distant memory.

Gradually, all the walls had been repainted and much
of the furniture replaced. Bit by bit, the cottage was being
stamped with her own personality, although there were little things belonging to Amanda which she kept because
they brought back fond memories of her friend before
things had gone pear-shaped: pretty tins and boxes which
Amanda had been fond of collecting even as a kid; a couple of pictures in frames; two vases—they were all in the
larder waiting for a spot to be found in the cottage.

Forgiveness was a good place to be and she could feel
herself getting there.

Rosie pulled open the front door. Her heart swooped
and dived and did all sorts of ridiculous things inside her
as Angelo stepped over the threshold, already unbuttoning his shirt, to wrap her in an embrace.

"I've cooked for us," Rosie murmured, pulling back
rather than just succumbing on the spot to his powerful,
masculine physicality. "There's a vegetable dish I'm trying
out for the catering job I have next Wednesday." She scattered little butterfly kisses on his mouth and laughed when
he pulled her forcefully towards him with a low growl.

"I'm not sure I can hold off until I've tasted the trial

vegetable dish." He moved against her so that she was left in no doubt that he was heavily aroused.

"We don't have to have sex as soon as you walk through the front door," Rosie muttered in the first small show of rebellion since they had fallen back into bed together six weeks ago. "I mean, we can actually have a glass of wine and some dinner, and maybe even watch a little television. There's a show I want to see about wildlife."

Angelo frowned. He had not expected this to last as long as it had, nor had he predicted that he would still be hot for her after weeks of losing himself at will in her succulent, sexily responsive body. Weaning himself off her was taking its time. Indulging in domestic cosiness wasn't going to help the process.

"I'll try the new dish," he drawled. "But watching telly isn't going to work for me."

Rosie held her smile and shrugged. "It was just a thought—" holding the smile made her jaws ache "—but you're right." She wound her arms up and around his neck. "Watching telly is a waste of valuable time."

Angelo gave a grunt of satisfaction and hoisted her off her feet to take her upstairs.

"One day you're going to do something to your back doing stuff like this." Rosie was laughing breathlessly and unbuttoning his shirt, which was difficult, as she was bounced up the stairs as though she weighed nothing.

"And will you play nurse and make me all better?" Angelo glanced down at her and their eyes tangled.

There were times, too many to count, when all he could see was the girl he had taken to his bed three years ago. Then, he had to remind himself of the woman lurking behind the girl, the schemer who had so nearly conned him into a relationship which would have eventually ended in tears because sooner or later he would have found out what she was all about. He had been spared that outcome, but he had to keep reminding himself of its existence, especially when, like now, her laughing, teasing eyes made something wrench inside him.

He was, by now, very familiar with the cottage. Her bedroom was the one directly above the small kitchen. She had made him put up an old-fashioned, flowery porcelain coat-hook behind the door and he knew that if he turned round her bathrobe would be hanging there.

Two weeks ago he had bought her a new bathrobe to replace the one she had, which was falling to pieces. Hell, it was only one thing, practically without value; she certainly wouldn't be able to pawn it for thousands of pounds! Where was the harm in that? She was his woman, at least for the time being, and as such he would rather not be affronted by the sight of her in something that should have been consigned to the dustbin years ago. It made complete sense. What *wouldn't* have made sense was the delicate jewellery box with the stained-glass sides and the diamond beading which he had happened to see in passing a few days previously. He was extremely glad he had resisted the temptation to buy it for her.

"I've never been good at nursing," Rosie quipped lightly, when she wanted to tell him that, yes, she would love nothing more than to take care of him, to have him spend a night in the cottage with her instead of dashing off whatever the time, as though he would turn into a pumpkin if he didn't. Rosie wasn't a fool. She knew exactly what this was all about, just as she knew that if she started trying to make more of it than it really was then he would disappear in a puff of smoke and she wasn't ready for that.

As he deposited her on the bed, her heart picked up speed as she wondered when she would *ever* be ready for him to disappear in a puff of smoke. She had dumped her reservations and jettisoned her misgivings to climb back into bed with him and now, as the need to hold him close and really talk to him swelled inside her, she was realising that she had made a colossal mistake. She had kidded herself that she was like him, that she could have sex with him and clear him out of her system once and for all. She had been a fool, because she was more embedded in this than ever before. Sleeping with Angelo was not diminishing her desire, it was stoking it.

Like it or not, she was at his mercy, as useless as a piece of flotsam bobbing along dependent for its direction on the ocean currents.

"Not true," Angelo admonished, half-smiling as he got undressed. "I distinctly remember you sorting out a cut on my finger once upon a time."

He frowned, annoyed with himself for having taken the conversation into the past. He never had, not even when he had sensed her trying to engineer it in that direction. He might occasionally have to remind himself of the sort of woman she really was, and of the reasons he had chosen to bring her back into his life, but the past remained out of bounds, a taboo subject.

"Sorting out cut fingers goes hand in hand with cooking." Rosie continued to keep it light while she chewed over the dawning horror that somehow feelings she had had for him, which had never gone away, were clawing their way back to the surface, ignoring all common sense and wreaking havoc with her pride, which insisted that she play the game the way he was playing it.

"There are all sorts of rules and regulations concerning cuts in the kitchen!" she chirruped, while feasting her eyes on the magnificent sight of his body. How could she still care about someone who didn't want her? How could those feelings stubbornly persist in the face of his emotional detachment? How could she long for a man who closed up every time the conversation became too personal? Who walked away, back to his own house at the end of every evening, when once they would spend nights together, making love whenever they woke up. A man who would one day tire of her, who would consider his appetite satisfied and who would stroll off into the horizon without a backward glance to find another woman, possibly a woman he would truly care about.

"Would you believe me if I told you that I wasn't all that interested in the rules and regulations of what happens in a kitchen?" He settled on the bed, straddled her glorious, supine body, offered himself to her and arched back as she took him in her mouth. He had his hand behind her head, fingers clasped in her hair. When she did this, his mind always went blank. Only she knew how to do this, to take him out of his body and transport him to another place, another time, another whole dimension.

He removed himself before he could topple over the edge and eased himself along the length of her body. When she had lived in London, she had never exercised. Now, however, she had started jogging round the lanes. He was always in danger of being dragged along for the ride, despite his frequent protests that there were other far more pleasurable forms of exercise. He now knew more about the landscape of where he owned his house than he ever had. Thanks to her jogging, her body, always slender, had become highly toned and he could feel the firmness of her stomach as he tasted the salty tanginess of her perspiration. He spread apart her legs and buried himself in the apex between them, licking and teasing until she was groaning underneath him.

He had laid down all the ground rules for this strange thing they had going on between them, and she was assiduous in obeying them. Which was exactly what he wanted, naturally, but he had to admit to himself that it gave him a kick of immense satisfaction when he could feel her lose control as he explored her body. Just as she was doing now as he sucked the honeyed moistness between her legs.

When he looked up, he could see her small breasts pointing upwards, nipples pinched, and it was a massive turn-on as she looked down at him and then deliberately took one nipple between her fingers so that she could tease it, rubbing it and pinching it until he had no option but to rise up so that he could brush aside her hand and put his mouth where it had been.

He could feel her ribcage under his palm and the beating of her heart. He suckled fiercely on one nipple, loving the sense of timeless peace it gave him. He could stay there for ever, tasting her, quietly going crazy with the anticipation of entering her and feeling her tightness wrap around him.

When neither of them could stand it any longer, he straightened, and for one fleeting moment, caught up in the momentum of the moment and gripped by a passion that made his whole body feel as though it was burning up, Angelo was tempted to forgo the contraception. She had suggested going on the pill. He had shrugged and told her that she could if she wanted, but there was no way he would be taking any chances so he would carry on using protection. He trusted no one but himself.

He knew that she was leaving the whole business of contraception to him and it rocked him even to allow the thought of taking a chance to find space in his head. And yet it had.

"Two seconds," he breathed roughly, reaching across her to the bedside drawer where he now left a packet of condoms.

Rosie wriggled up, licked his rigid shaft and felt him

shudder and still as he did his utmost to control the need to spill his seed over her.

Then, with a little sigh and closing her eyes, she lay back down as he thrust into her, fully protected, taking no chances.

Their bodies moved to the same soaring rhythm. She could feel every inch of him in her, moving and pushing and bringing her closer and closer to orgasm. There were times when he was down there, between her legs, teasing her with his mouth, when she couldn't hold on and, wonderful though it was to come against his mouth, having him in her was pure ecstasy. Her nails dug into his back. Hands on either side of her, he pushed himself up so that he could increase the friction between them. She wrapped her legs around his waist and lost herself in the moment, soaring higher and higher until she cried out and gave in to the long, shuddering climax and the ripples and waves in its aftermath.

"Very nice." Angelo sighed with unhidden satisfaction as they both subsided, fully replete. He pulled her to him so that her head was resting on his chest, just how he liked it; this way he could stroke her hair and he enjoyed the fine, silky texture sifting through his fingers.

"Is that all you can say? Nice is such an *ordinary* word."

"Very earth-shattering, if you prefer."

"I shall have to get up in a minute. I have those vegetables to see about. I don't suppose you're interested in hearing how I intend to cook them?"

"Not in the slightest."

"Well, I'm going to steam them in the usual way, but then I'm going to refine the dish with some coconut milk, curry powder and cheese. Hopefully they'll be spot-on by the time I perfect them and I won't have to endure John Law in the kitchen pretending to be a chef when all he wants to do is…well…you know… Pretty disgusting, when his wife is outside chivvying the hired help into dressing the table just the way she likes it."

Rosie reluctantly sidled off the bed and, with her back to Angelo, she missed his sudden stillness.

"No. I don't know. Tell me."

Rosie glanced over her shoulder to find his eyes on her and she gave a little shrug of her shoulders.

"You met me when I was a waitress in a cocktail bar. You know the kind of thing I'm talking about."

Angelo could feel white-hot fury building in him like a volcano but he kept his voice calm and neutral.

"Who is this John Law character?" He could have destroyed her stalker at a whim. He had chosen not to because the threat of ruin was sometimes even more powerful than actual ruin itself. John Law? A married man? Making a play behind *his* woman? Threat of destruction almost seemed too good for any man like that.

"Oh, just someone who hired me a couple of weeks ago to cater a dinner party." Rosie had wandered off into the bathroom. Angelo heard the sound of the shower but for once he had no desire to join her under it.

"And he and his wife have asked me to cater for another dinner party in a few days' time!" she called, stepping under the shower when it became apparent that he wasn't going to join her.

"How do you get back from these things?" Angelo had made his way into the bathroom, and through the frosted glass he could make out her long, slender shape as she vigorously soaped herself and shampooed her hair. He slung a towel round his hips, closed the lid of the toilet, sat there.

"What?" Rosie poked her head around the shower door and looked at him.

"Simple question, Rosie. How do you travel back from these dos that you cater for at night? You don't have a car."

"I know. It's a nuisance but I just can't afford to buy one at the moment." She switched off the shower and stepped out, riffling her fingers through her wet hair and then drying herself as he continued to watch her with brooding, lazy intensity. "I'm doing pretty well at the moment. In fact, better than I thought I would be. There are lots of rich people in this part of the world, and not nearly as many people around to cater to their needs as there are in London. But I've still had to put out quite a bit of money for kitchen equipment. Also, the decorating took a chunk out of my savings."

"You're not answering my question."

"What's wrong?" She paused, frowned at him and then stalked out of the bathroom, back into the bedroom to change into some fresh clothes. She was beginning to feel nervous but that was something she didn't intend to share with him. Had she done something wrong? She hated questioning herself, saw no reason for it, yet she was. They had made love, and it had been brilliant, but he hadn't jumped into the shower with her the way he usually did; hadn't reminded her of his insatiable appetite while they were dripping wet under the water. And the way he was staring at her now…

She slipped on her jogging bottoms, rolled them twice at the waistband so that they rode down low on her slim hips, doing this with her back to him just in case she saw something in his face she didn't want to see. She could feel herself getting angry because she hated the helplessness that overwhelmed her whenever she thought of him ending what they had.

"What makes you think that there's something wrong?"

"I'm not an idiot, Angelo. Why does it matter how I

travel to work or back from work? Why are you making such a big deal of this?" *Unless it's a cover for something else. Unless you're trying to engineer an argument so that you can use it as an excuse to break up...*

"Tell me more about this John Law character." Angelo flung aside the towel, strode to the shower and turned the water to cold, which he thought might lower the temperature raging inside him. He didn't look at her as he emerged a minute later to resume the conversation.

"He and his wife, Jayne, were one of my first customers," Rosie explained. "They live about half an hour away in one of the large new-build houses on that estate by the river."

"What does the man do? Aside from making passes at you?"

Rosie's brain sluggishly began to grasp what was going on and her eyes widened. "Are you... *jealous?*"

"Have you done anything for me to be jealous about?" Angelo's face darkened as he stared at her. "Do you reciprocate when he's touching you, as he stands in front of the chocolate mousse making helpful suggestions?"

"I'm not going to bother answering that question." She began swinging out of the room and he reached out, caught her arm and pulled her back against him.

"What does he do?"

"Angelo, you're over-reacting. He makes the odd remark and he leers a bit, but he's never *touched* me, and if he did I would know how to take care of myself. And how can you suggest that I would ever *do anything* with someone else? Do you think I would be sleeping with you if...if...?" *If there was the slightest chance that I could feel something, anything, for someone else? Do you think I wouldn't run as fast as I could in the opposite direction from you if I*

*could because I know you're going to hurt me? If I hadn't
gone and fallen madly in love with you all over again?*

"If what?"

"If nothing. Let me go, Angelo. I'm going to go downstairs to start doing some food. If you want to eat here,
then fine, but if you're going to start arguing with me over
nothing then I would rather you left."

It was the first argument they had, and Rosie knew that
if she tolerated him trying to dictate to her then she would
set the precedent. She was in his thrall sufficiently as it
was, without becoming even more feeble and pathetic. He
had no right to question her integrity and if he was jealous,
which he surely wasn't, then it didn't spring from any tender loving feelings. It sprang from the fact that, whilst they
were in this situation, he considered her his possession to
be tossed aside as and when he chose, like a toy he could
discard when he got sick of playing with it.

She took the stairs two at a time and wasn't aware of him
following her until she looked around to see him lounging
indolently in the doorway. He had dressed in a pair of jeans
and a faded T-shirt. He always carried a change of clothes
with him when he came down from London and he always
took them with him when he left. Her heart lurched but
she looked at him coolly and with complete composure.

"So I believe you when you tell me that the man hasn't
laid a finger on you nor you on him," Angelo gritted. Just
the thought of anyone else touching her made his blood
boil. He should have paid more attention to her job. He
should have realised that she would be coming into contact
with lots of different people, lots of *rich* people, and she
was nothing if not susceptible to men with deep pockets,
he grimly told himself. Furthermore, she was sex on legs,
even with her hair half-wet as it was now and completely
devoid of make-up. In the world of the rich and the beau-

tiful, her natural, pure beauty stood out like a beacon in the darkness. Of course there would be lechers wanting to grope her over the minestrone soup. Hell, why had that never crossed his mind? He suddenly would have liked details of every man she had encountered at every party she had catered since she had moved to Cornwall. He raked his fingers through his dark hair and glowered.

"Good. I'm glad to hear it." Rosie stubbornly stuck her chin out and glowered back.

"You're here in this place on your own without transport. It's remote. So who wouldn't be worried about *anyone* in a situation like that?"

"You're worried about me?"

"I think you should get a car," Angelo prevaricated. "And you never answered my question."

"I've forgotten what the question was."

"How do you get to and from these events?"

"Beth has a little runaround—she's the girl who helps me now and again. So if we're working on a job together we'll always drive there in her car, and if she leaves before me in the evening then I call a taxi."

"So you don't accept lifts from any of those creeps who try to manhandle you?" He fought to get a grip but still found himself scowling darkly at her.

Rosie turned away and laughed lightly. She didn't want to give house room to that warm feeling she got when she thought of him being jealous and possessive over her. "You know my background, Angelo. I wasn't born yesterday. I know what men can be like. I value the jobs I get here, and there's no way I would ever jeopardise any of that by accepting a lift from someone who might make a pass at me. One client who's pregnant at the moment and not drinking has given me a lift twice, and that's okay, but I know where to draw the line."

"You should still get a car."

"I'll carry on saving."

He wasn't going to offer to buy one for her. No way. Been there, done that, when it came to buying things for her. He decided not to think of her travelling back in winter, when the days would get shorter and shorter. Hell, he probably wouldn't even be with the woman when winter rolled round!

He continued to look at her in brooding silence as she began expertly preparing the vegetables.

"So who else do you meet at these things?" He had only arranged that one, initial catering job. It had mushroomed into lots of other catering jobs and he had no idea who those jobs were for.

"Lots of different people." Rosie shrugged. "Do you want to help me with these vegetables?"

It didn't occur to Angelo that chopping carrots and peeling potatoes fell into the category of domestic. He was too busy speculating on these mysterious and unknown people who now comprised her social life.

"What sort of people? You can't be too careful."

"I think I'm fine."

"And yet you're the same woman who mistakenly went on a date with a psychopath."

"One mistake, Angelo. It's not very fair of you to remind me of that." Rosie began chopping some cloves of garlic very quickly.

"I'm making an obvious point."

"Which is what? That I'm not equipped to take care of myself? That's a far cry from the nasty gold-digger I'm supposed to be, isn't it?"

Angelo flushed darkly. "Is it a problem for you that I'm expressing concern for your safety?"

Rosie laughed incredulously. "Angelo, this is a quiet,

middle-class rural area in Cornwall. Not a war zone in the Middle East!"

Angelo didn't like where this was going. He didn't like his own biting curiosity. He didn't care for the flare of jealousy he felt when he thought of her being ogled by strangers. It would be a relief when he was free of her once and for all. Despite the fact that he called the shots, he sometimes got the unnerving feeling that he really wasn't in control at all and that was a feeling he didn't like.

He curved his hand at the side of her neck and bent to kiss the slender column. Her hair smelled fresh and fruity and he gently raised some of the strands so that he could nibble her hairline until she squirmed with pleasure.

"You're tickling!"

"I don't like to think of anyone coming near you."

"Not even the pregnant lady who gave me the lift?"

"You know what I mean."

"I meet people. It's a social job. Rich women who want dinner parties catered for tend to be married to rich men."

"Rich *old* men?" Still kissing her neck, he wrapped his arms around her before slipping his hands under her top, moving slowly upwards until he was cupping her small, perfect breasts. With her back to him, he pressed his body against her so that she could feel the hardness of his erection.

"Ancient and wrinkled." Rosie flattened herself against him and quivered when he circled her nipples with his fingers. In a heartbeat, she had forgotten all her negative thoughts about him and about what he was capable of doing to her. She widened her stance, and on cue he dipped his hand under the soft elastic of her jogging bottoms, wormed his fingers beneath her underwear and then idly began playing with her.

She groaned softly when his fingers found the pouting bud of her clitoris. She was wet and hot for him. How was it fair that he could do this to her? The one consoling thought was that she could also do the same to him. He was as rampant as she was, and as impatient for them to make love all over again, as though they hadn't finished making love less than an hour ago.

He eased the jogging bottoms down and, before they could pool round her ankles, he turned her to face him.

In one easy movement, he lifted her up and set her gently down on the kitchen table. She lay flat, barely noticing the hard surface of the wood under her. When she bent her knees, her feet were half-on, half-off the edge of the kitchen table, and when he divested her of the jogging bottoms she was spread wide like a ripe peach waiting to be savoured.

"I still have to cook," she protested weakly, but her eyelids fluttered shut and she gave herself over to the intense pleasure of his tongue exploring, licking and rasping against her sensitised clitoris until she wanted to scream out loud. She kept her hands tightly clasped behind her back and fought against the urge to buck until she climaxed.

Angelo knew just how far to take her before pulling away and this time he took her to that place over and over again until she was begging him, *pleading* with him, to enter her.

When he finally removed his mouth to insert himself in her, he was as desperate for release as she was. He coiled his fingers in her hair and thrust powerfully, pushing her back slightly, repeating the thrusts until she could no longer fight the irresistible need to give in to her orgasm.

"I don't want you looking at anyone," he rasped in harsh, uneven bursts as he thrust one final time deep into her.

"And I don't want anyone looking at *you!* I don't like the thought of it. It angers me."

Rosie bit down her words. She wanted to scream out loud that she couldn't imagine looking at anyone but him. She remembered a time when she would have had no hesitation in telling him that, in looking at him with openly adoring eyes. She had been the tough girl from the wrong side of the tracks who had turned to mush in his hands. Now, she kept silent, but she was breathing in small, gasping moans as he withdrew from her. She felt as weak as a kitten and it was a few seconds before she could even think of raising herself up on the table to shakily grope around for the jogging bottoms. Her top was still on. They hadn't even managed to make it to fully undressed mode.

When she fully surfaced from her languorous, pleasurable stupor, it was to find him staring out of the kitchen window with his back to her, as rigid as a plank of wood.

Like her, he hadn't fully undressed and his jeans were back on, though as he slowly turned around the trousers were still unzipped and unbuttoned.

She clocked the expression on his face and said hesitantly, "What's the matter?"

"I didn't use protection," Angelo told her bluntly. "I don't know what the hell happened there, but I forgot to take precautions."

"Oh."

"More than just *oh,*" he gritted.

"Okay! I know you think that it would be a disaster if I fell pregnant…"

"Disaster is putting it mildly."

"But you can stop worrying. I'm one-hundred-percent safe." And she was, but once again she knew that the time was coming for her to deal with this situation. How could he be possessive one minute and then dismissive the next?

How could lover and stranger be so close to one another? How much did he really hate her?

"And I wouldn't want a pregnancy any more than you," she added coldly. "When I get pregnant, it will be with someone I want to spend the rest of my life with. Someone who wants to spend the rest of his life with me. So you don't have to tell me that it would be worse than a disaster if the person to make me pregnant were ever to be you."

CHAPTER EIGHT

"WHAT DID YOU expect?" he asked irritably. "That I would be overjoyed that we forgot to take precautions?" He retired to the kitchen table and sat on one of the chairs, turning it to face her and dragging another over so that he could use it as a foot-rest. He waited for her to tell him that chairs were for bottoms and not feet and her failure to say the obvious was proof enough of her mood.

"You don't have to keep reminding me. You said it once. I got the message loud and clear."

"Are you telling me that you object? That you would actually *want* to get pregnant?" His voice was duly appalled although for the first time he wondered what she would look like pregnant. He would bet that she would show almost immediately. She was very slender. He squashed the inappropriate thought, angry with himself for even allowing it to enter his mind in the first place.

"I told you I wouldn't and I meant it." Rosie slammed the Aga door and wiped her hands on her apron which she then proceeded to remove. She faced him squarely, her warm, brown eyes clashing with his deep sea-green ones. She was bombarded with tumultuous emotions: anger with herself for still loving him despite everything; anger with him for the conversations he refused to have; the questions he refused to broach and the implications he insisted on making.

She wanted to hit him for being so brutally, cruelly blunt with her, yet she had to stop herself from straying closer towards him, from relinquishing herself to that charmed, irresistible zone that seemed to operate around him. Without trying, he could take a sledgehammer to her defences and smash them to smithereens.

"There's a guy somewhere out there for me and that's the person I'm saving myself for," she added, because if he wanted to make his messages loud and clear then why shouldn't she? Even if the message was a complete lie, because she couldn't imagine that there could be anyone out here worth saving herself for aside from him.

Angelo was outraged that she should even be thinking along those lines when she was sleeping with him. Once again, he found himself wondering about those people she met in the daily course of her life catering for the rich and successful. Maybe he should get her to cater for *him,* if only to prove that when it came to rich and successful, he was as good as it got. Add sex into the equation and she wouldn't be standing there in front of him, hands on her hips, yammering on about the perfect guy waiting out there for her.

"If I remember correctly," he inserted smoothly, "*I* was that guy not a hundred years ago."

"That was before you dumped me without hearing what I had to say and made off with my best friend."

Angelo shrugged. "I'm not going to be drawn into a pointless discussion of the past."

"Because of your stupid ground rules for this so-called *relationship* of ours? If you would just let me explain…" So the whole episode with the wretched pawn tickets might not show her up in the best possible light but she was beyond caring. She should have explained the situation from the start. But what was the good of beating herself up over things that should or shouldn't have been done?

"I told you. Not interested."

"Why not?"

"It wasn't just about you selling the things I was stupid enough to give you, Rosie."

Rosie went perfectly still. For three years she had thought that her silly mistake, her wretched stupidity in not coming clean with Angelo, had been the only ammunition Amanda had used against her. What else could there possibly have been? She could hear her heart beating like a drum inside her as she frantically tried to work out what he was trying to say.

"And we're not going there," Angelo informed her, his expression cool and remote.

"How can you tell me something like that and then refuse to elaborate?"

"It's easier than you think."

"It's not easy for *me!*" Rosie cried. "You've opened up a whole new can of worms."

"I didn't open anything. I merely had the lot dumped in my lap, and I'm telling you that pawning my presents wasn't the complete story." He strolled towards her, unsmiling. "If you really want to pursue this," he told her softly, "then I'm out of here."

"What do you mean?"

"I told you from the start that this isn't about us rehashing the past. What happened, happened and there's no going back to that place. This is about sex. Nothing more. If you can't live with that, then I'm going to walk out of that door and you'll never set eyes on me again."

Angelo knew that this was precisely what he should be doing—taking control. Holding on to the reins of this situation. At odds with that certainty, was the sudden sickening, swooping feeling inside him at the prospect of her taking him at his word and showing him the door. Of course, this was no sign of vulnerability. He didn't *do* vulnerable!

"Is that what you want?" he pressed, in the same low, soft voice, barely a murmur. "When the sex is still so good between us?"

"How can you be so…so…*disconnected*?"

"I deal with facts. The fact is that what we have here, the chemistry that's still between us, is good and I want to carry on exploring it but without complications. If you can't see your way past the complications, then there's only one option left for us."

The protests rose up in Rosie's throat. There were so many questions she wanted to ask. But how would life be if he walked out the door? He would. There was no question about that. He might want her, but he wasn't emotionally invested, and if he weighed up the pros and cons and the scales weren't to his liking then he wouldn't hesitate to leave her all over again.

She recognised her own weakness and hated it, but how could those questions ever be answered if he disappeared? If he walked away, she would forever wonder what else had turned him off her. What else Amanda might have said to push the destruct button on their relationship. Not to mention the glaringly obvious truth, which was that she physically couldn't get enough of him. She had given up trying to kid herself that by sleeping with him she would somehow, magically, work him out of her system. That trick would work for him but not for her. Instead, she would be left with a gaping hole in her life. What was wrong with being greedy and just taking what was on offer for as long as it was on offer? What was wrong in not being a martyr?

And, besides, things changed. One day he might just break his self-imposed silence and provide her with the answer to yet one more question plaguing her. Wasn't it worth it to keep this going, to hope that he might just open up and talk to her, give her the opportunity to defend herself? It might be his last parting shot but it would be worth it. For him, unfinished business would be done and dusted when he was sick of sleeping with her, tired and bored of bedding the one woman he had been prematurely forced to jettison. For her, unfinished business could only ever be finished when she had heard what else had been said about her, when she had had the chance to air her point of view.

"I need to check the vegetables in the Aga," she said stiffly, lowering her eyes so that she couldn't witness the flare of triumph on his face. When she sneakily glanced up at him, there was no triumph there and he was right behind her. Instead, he gently ran his finger along the side of her face. The gesture was so tender that she had to gulp back tears.

Angelo knew that he had won. The relief nearly knocked him off his feet. She was his. Could that be called sweet revenge? Strangely, the concept of revenge couldn't have been further from his mind.

"Okay. So tell me all about these people you cater for. Do they pay the bills?"

"I'm doing okay." Rosie moved away. With her back to him, she chatted about her days, about the meals she had cooked, about some of her quirky customers, about all the stuff she knew he wanted to hear. Inconsequential stuff that papered over the big issues at the heart of their relationship which he had no intention of dealing with.

"And you don't miss the bright lights at all?" He hadn't realised how much he enjoyed the way she talked to him, without any of the ingratiating subservience he encountered pretty much every day from everyone in his life.

"I yearn for night clubs and bars," she said, reluctantly laughing at the outright lie.

"You're welcome to dip your feet there if you want. Say the word and you can always come down to London for a night. I have a range of apartments you could use."

Just so long as she didn't get it into her head that sharing *his* apartment was an option, Rosie thought, reading between the lines.

"Of course," he added casually, "you'll have to take me along for the ride." He began helping her set the table. He no longer had to think where to find things. He knew where everything was, from the mismatched plates which she had brought with her, to the impractical silver cutlery she had bought three weeks ago at the boot sale she had dragged him to. Who wanted to waste valuable time polishing cutlery? he had asked her. Wasn't that an outdated practice that had rightly died a death a few decades back? She had ignored him.

"That might be awkward." Rosie kept it light as she dug into the chicken and vegetables on her plate. Perfect; definitely to be tried out on her next customer in a week's time. "What if I come across my ideal guy and you're there lurking in the corner to spoil my party?"

Angelo grinned, although the effort hurt his jaw. "The same might be said for me."

"Do you have an ideal woman?"

"I could think of a few winning traits."

Rosie didn't want to pursue this. She imagined that one of those winning traits would be resisting the temptation to pawn the gifts he bought her, whatever the driving necessity to do so. Along with not doing whatever she was supposed to have done in addition.

Angelo said lazily, changing the subject, "I'm considering hiring you to do some catering for me."

"Because you think that I mightn't be making sufficient money?"

"Because your vegetables are the best I've ever eaten."

"You're kidding, right?"

"Why so shocked?"

"I don't need a helping hand."

Angelo wondered how she would react if he informed her that she had already had one of those. "Roughly a hundred people. Can you rise to the occasion?"

"A hundred?"

"Too many? Some locals. Some important clients. Quite a few from my head office who deserve to be royally rewarded for the past six months of gruelling workload."

Rosie's eyes lit up. She began planning menus in her head. This vote of confidence was really significant because Angelo would never have thought of using her if he didn't rate her food. He might enjoy sleeping with her but he was no pushover when it came to good value for his money. Ever since he had casually told her about where he came from, she could see that money was not something he ever took for granted.

"I'll have to have at least three girls helping me for that number of people," she said thoughtfully. "Will you want me to arrange waiting staff as well?"

"The lot. We can talk money when you've got your menu and shown it to me."

"Where is the venue?"

"You haven't seen my house yet, have you?" He knew that he was straying from his own ground rules. He hadn't planned on taking her to his mansion, even though out of sight, and surrounded by a barrier of sweeping conifers, it was within a stone's throw of the cottage. He had determined from day one that her greedy little eyes would not clock its vastness, not to mention the eminently saleable items liberally scattered everywhere. Why leave pound coins lying around if there was a thief in the house?

"No, I haven't. I haven't even gone for any walks in that direction." Just in case he started thinking that she was remotely interested.

Angelo refrained from passing the obviously caustic rejoinder.

"And when do you have in mind?" Rosie asked, all business.

"We can get down to the details later," Angelo murmured. "Right now, I need to work off all the calories from that meal." After their near disagreement, he relished the delighted flush in her cheeks at his catering suggestion. He was a man who planned life down to the final letter but sometimes, he could now concede, a touch of spontaneity was worth a thousand words.

"There were very few calories in that meal." She went to the drawer where she kept all her business paraphernalia. "I'm experimenting with healthy-eating options and low-cal alternatives."

"Fascinating."

"Maybe not for you, because you don't need to lose weight."

"Is that your way of telling me that I'm a perfect specimen?"

"I can give you some basic costs right now. Of course, I'll prepare a proper invoice, and you can rest assured that I have all the necessary insurance."

More than anything else, Rosie wanted to prove to him that he was no longer an indispensable part of her life. Not the way he once had been. She might be putty in his hands when it came to the physical side of things, but it was very important that she show him how independent she was in all other respects.

Which was why, a fortnight later, everything she would need for his party was ready, prepared and awaiting transport on the eve of the big day. She had no idea what to expect. She knew that most of her current clients were going to be attending the event. They appeared to be bristling with excitement. Social diaries were being altered, previous engagements cancelled and long-standing friends postponed so that the party of the year wouldn't be missed.

By now, Rosie was on sufficiently good terms with some of the locals, clients and non-clients, that she was privy to the interesting fact that Angelo had all but abandoned his mansion over the past few years. She reckoned that that would have had something to do with Amanda's occasional presence in the cottage, although she had kept that to herself.

She was waiting for Beth, her main helper and now her friend who was her right-hand person at many of her catering events, when she heard the sound of cars pulling into the narrow drive: an old banger and behind it a sleek, low-slung silver sports car. Rosie's eyes popped out and her mouth fell open when she saw Angelo manoeuvring himself out of the old banger with a great degree of difficulty.

"Amazing," he said. "My sports car is the size of a matchbox and yet I don't emerge from it feeling as though my legs have been broken in three places."

"What's going on?" Outside, it was a fine summer's afternoon with a perfectly cloudless blue sky. Rosie hadn't yet donned her catering outfit, which was usually a pair of black trousers and a white shirt: smart, practical and fairly timeless. Instead, she was in a vest and a pair of loose harem trousers. Her feet had been hastily shoved into a pair of old flip flops.

"A couple of hundred quid," Angelo drawled, walking towards her while his driver, as she could now see, remained in the sports car. "I called in a small favour."

"You're not making any sense." The car was a peculiar

shade of yellow, an ancient little box, more like a small
van than a car.

"You're doing my catering. I've got you a car. And don't
bother to thank me. Like I said, it barely cost a penny, but
I've been told that the engine's tuned up to within an inch
of its life and it runs well. One careful female owner."

"You bought this for *me?*"

"Make sure the house is back to its original state by the
time I leave tomorrow and you can consider the car ade-
quate recompense, in addition to the hourly rate we agreed
for your services."

Rosie opened her mouth to reject his gift, to tell him that
she wasn't about to accept a car from him, however much
he downplayed its value. But it would be very useful, and
she knew that if he had sourced it there would be no sin-
ister engine problems waiting to spring to light the second
she had handed over her cash. And she liked the way it
looked. It had character. She smiled and hesitantly walked
around it, running her hand along the side and peering in
to the old-fashioned walnut dashboard and the weird gear
stick which she would have to get used to.

The kick of satisfaction Angelo got as he covertly looked
at her expressive face was immense. How did it make sense
that the expensive gifts he had once given her, which she
had promptly taken to the pawnbrokers, had never generated such genuine, appreciative warmth on her face?

He was momentarily disconcerted by an intense longing to hear what she had to say about all that stuff she had
hocked, why she had done it—then he remembered the
other reason he had walked away from her and he closed
his mind off to the dangerous pull of curiosity.

"She's wonderful," Rosie said simply. "Thank you."

Angelo flushed. "If it breaks down, you're on your own.

I don't fix cars and I wouldn't expect the guy I bought it from to turn into your personal mechanic."

"It was a kind gesture." She smiled at him. Did he know how much deeper he burrowed into the heart of her when he did something like this? When his hostility was buried underneath something other than the sheets on a bed? He was so cold-blooded in his aim to have her as his plaything, a willing sexual object to be used until he grew tired of her. Yet, if there had been nothing more than that, then wouldn't she also be on the road to recovery?

Instead, he did this, bought her this old jalopy which was worthless and priceless at the same time. He allowed himself to be dragged to markets and he helped with the dishes whilst informing her that he would never spend the night or waste time watching television, insisting on retiring to his mansion up the lane. Couldn't he see that in lots of other ways he was getting to her more successfully than if he *did* watch a cookery channel with her? Or accidentally fell asleep and spent the night? Ordering her to keep still so that he could trap a spider by her leg, as he had done two weekends ago, carried the sound of the key turning to unlock her heart ever faster.

He didn't look as though he was particularly thrilled with her remark about his kindness, although as he glanced away she felt that he wasn't displeased.

"I'll expect you at the house by six," he told her gruffly, walking towards his own car and slipping into the passenger seat next to his driver. "And don't be late. I don't tolerate lateness in my employees."

In fact, she was there by five-thirty. By six-thirty the kitchen was fragrant with the smells of dishes simmering. On the massive central island, platter upon platter of crudités were laid out, ready to be served. The three girls helping her could barely contain themselves. Despite being given a strict dress code similar to hers of black trousers and a smart white blouse, they had showed up in small black skirts and white tops that seemed suspiciously too small and had all exchanged puzzled, innocent looks when reprimanded.

By seven, the first of the many guests began to arrive. Some were being chauffeured down, others were taking advantage of the limo service from the station to the house. Nothing had been discussed about her role beyond caterer and she understood from Angelo's silence on the subject that she would be there as a background facilitator, making sure that the food was perfect and the service faultless. Would she even be introduced to guests? She certainly wouldn't be in the role as his lover!

But she couldn't contain a growing sense of frustration mingled with vague disappointment and hurt as she continued to give her all during the course of the evening—hustling the girls, overseeing the delivery of the food from kitchen to dining room, arranging the layout as attractively as possible—while only glimpsing Angelo in snatches. She felt hot, bothered and irritated because surely the least she could have expected would have been for her employer to actually take an interest in what she was doing?

But he was busy, wrapped up talking finance with the movers and shakers of the business community. She saw him standing with a drink in his hand, surrounded by men who were nodding and agreeing with whatever he was saying.

She glimpsed him helping himself to canapés and chatting to several of the local women who had surrounded him like ants round nectar. A few times he caught her eye but made no move to come across. She had lost count of the number of people arriving and was only glad that she had been wise enough to over- rather than under-cater.

By eleven, she was beginning to think that she was well worth the jalopy he had generously presented to her. This was the largest number of people she had ever catered for. It was a blessing that she had managed to share the preparation with Beth, whose kitchen was twice the size of hers. Even bearing in mind that the dishes had all been brought prepared but uncooked to his house, she still felt that it was a triumph of what could be done with hard work and a clever menu that was delicious but uncomplicated.

She had hired a team of waiting staff to constantly re-fill glasses. She had suggested and sourced a jazz quartet who were a beautiful addition to the evening. She had even been responsible for the subtle lighting in the various rooms because there was nothing less welcoming than the harsh glare of bright overhead lights.

And had he seen fit to thank her? Far too busy! Had he come over *once* to congratulate her on her efforts? Too tied up!

Hassled, she finally decided to hunt him down as midnight approached and there was no sign of the party wrapping up. She told herself that it was essential to talk to him about arrangements for cleaning up. They surely couldn't all be expected to hang around until the last guest decided that it was either time to leave or retire to one of the many bedrooms which would be put to use over the weekend.

She saw him in silhouette. Outside, lanterns illuminated the extensive stepped patio at the back of the house. They offered a tantalising glimpse of sprawling manicured lawns which, through all his years of absence from the house, had continued to be groomed by a fleet of experienced gardeners. She had barely had time to appreciate its immensity and its splendour because as soon as she had arrived she had been called to duty.

And now, she couldn't possibly appreciate the view in a more flattering light, but she was oblivious to the scenery... She couldn't tear her eyes away from Angelo, who was lounging in the shadows against the wall, towering over a diminutive, curvaceous woman who had a cigarette clasped in one hand and a glass in the other. Their body language was telling. Rosie could feel the blood leech out of her face as she continued to stare...and stare...until he slowly raised his eyes to see her frozen by one of the ivy-clad romanesque columns just beyond the French doors.

Angelo didn't have to be a mind reader to realise what was going through Rosie's head. He hesitated. He wasn't entirely sure why he had allowed himself to be persuaded into "getting some fresh air" with Eleanor French, a sexy, high-powered lawyer, one of the members of the elite legal team used by his people to close his last, massive deal. He had never met her before but he had known what she was about the second she opened the conversation with a controversial take on a certain piece of recent legislation designed to demonstrate her IQ, while her challenging, coy looks were designed to demonstrate something else entirely.

Of course he had known that she would come on to him. He hadn't been born yesterday. Had he wanted that? Had he wanted to prove to himself that he could still be attracted to another woman, a woman whose physical charms were beyond dispute? Whose mind was challenging? The sort of woman any red-blooded man with half a brain would have been incapable of resisting? Had he wanted to prove to himself that the power Rosie seemed to have over him was an illusion? That no one who had conned, duped and taken him for a ride could have power over him, whatever the sexual pull?

The minute his eyes tangled with Rosie's, he felt a sharp jab of stirring satisfaction at the flare of primitive jealousy in her eyes. It was *tangible.*

"Excuse me," he murmured to the blonde, who could have been invisible as far as Angelo was concerned. Already Rosie was turning around and he was gripped with a sense of urgency which he successfully fought off.

"You'll be back? Shall I wait here for you to return?"

Angelo detected the beseeching, anxious tone in her voice with distaste.

"I wouldn't bother," he said, killing any further debate on the subject. He could have told her that he found her as appealing as mouldy cheese and that she would be far better off trying her charms out on a more receptive audience. Instead, he walked away, although Rosie was disappearing fast through the throng. He caught her just as she was about to hurry into the sanctuary of the busy kitchen.

"You were looking for me?" He pulled her aside into one of the smaller rooms which had not been opened for the party.

Rosie was on fire. What had he been doing out there? What had she interrupted? They had looked very cosy indeed. Had he met her before? Who *was* she anyway? Rosie couldn't bring herself to think that anything had happened between them, but had she witnessed the beginning of the end of what they, he and Rosie, had? Cold, clammy fear sank its teeth into her, making her feel sick and giddy.

"I've been rushed off my feet all evening. I just thought I'd go outside and take a few minutes' time out." Her cheeks were burning and she couldn't meet his eyes. The room he had pulled her into was a small snug, the least grand of all the rooms she had seen. It felt small and oppressive and the silence suddenly thick between them. Rosie clasped her hands tightly together.

Next to all the gloriously and elaborately dressed women out there strutting their stuff, next to the small blonde in the short dress smoking and flirting with Angelo, playing all those tried and tested games, Rosie was dully aware of the uninspiring sight she must make. Her face felt greasy and she had sensibly tied her hair back but she no longer had the sort of long hair that could easily be tied back. Strands hung limply against her face, and her outfit might be practical but it was bland and indifferent. Then again, she told herself, she was invisible, an employee, as he had made sure to demonstrate by ignoring her for the duration of the evening. She was his bit on the side, a little secret. It was sharply brought home to her how low down the pecking order she was in his estimation.

"Can I go now?" she asked politely, and Angelo frowned. It was neither the time nor the place but his hands itched to tug her hair free and to have her right here, right now, with the door shut and guests milling about outside.

"You're doing a good job," he said. "Correction—you *did* a good job, an excellent job. Everyone complimented the food and the evening went like clockwork. The jazz band was perfect."

"Thank you."

"Is that it?"

"What do you expect, Angelo?" Her eyes flashed and she tilted her head to glare at him. "You paid me to do a good job and I'm pleased that I did a good job, along with all the people who helped me. I know the food went down well because lots of people told me."

"And I didn't. Is that what you're trying to say?"

Rosie remained silent. She didn't want to sound as though she was whining. She was a professional and professionals didn't whinge because their employers were sparse in their praise.

"You were busy," she said eventually. She could feel his fabulous green eyes on her but she kept her face averted and stared fixedly at the open fireplace and the painting above it.

"Are you in a mood because you happened to see me outside with a woman?"

Rosie thought she could detect amusement in his voice, and anger flared like a firecracker exploding inside her, but she wasn't going to let it take her over. She gritted her teeth together and stubbornly refused to look at him.

"Well?" Angelo prompted. Through the closed door, the sound of the party outside was a muffled blur interspersed with laughter. He thought he might possibly be missed if they remained in the room any longer but he didn't really care. He was intrigued by the slow flush of colour spreading across her cheeks.

"Who was she?" This time, Rosie *did* look at him. If he tried lying, she would see right through it and the need to know was greater than the need to contain herself and feign indifference.

"You're jealous."

"I'm not going to be one of a number," Rosie said tightly. "You don't have to tell me that this isn't going to last, but whilst it's ongoing then I'm either the only woman you share a bed with or it's goodbye."

Angelo laughed mirthlessly. "I don't respond well to threats like that," he told her grimly. Suddenly *she* was full of scruples and moral principles? Hilarious. "I also don't do jealousy. That's not part of what we've got."

"I'm not jealous."

"Really? Because that's what I see written all over your face." He was saying all the right things, all the things he knew he should be saying, so why did he still want to push her up against the wall and make love to her until she was a quivering wreck? He could already feel his erection pushing painfully against his zip, big, bold and eager to feel the uniqueness of her body as he thrust into her.

"Then you need to get your eyes checked." But had he answered her question? No. Had he told her who the mystery blonde was? No. The walls of the snug seemed to be pressing down on her. She was suffocating. "If you can't even tell me who that woman is, and if all you can do is accuse me of being jealous and then give me a long lecture on jealousy not being part of the deal, then…"

"Then what?"

"I have to get back to the kitchen. There are liqueurs to be served. The staff will be starting to wonder where I've gone."

"Then *what?*"

Rosie knew that he was pressing her for an answer and she was afraid that she knew only too well what that meant—he wanted her to push him into a decision he had already made for himself. He wanted her to end it to spare him the trouble of ending it himself.

"Oh, for God's sake!" Angelo raked his fingers through his hair and looked at her with rampant frustration. "Okay, so she's a high-powered lawyer and the first time I met her was tonight."

Rosie wondered if it was possible to hear the sound of her relief. So he still didn't do jealousy, it was still one of the many things not allowed in the strange relationship they had, but he had answered her question. Mostly. She didn't say anything.

"And you went outside with her?"

Angelo was tempted to tell her that further cross-examination was out of the question. But then, at the end of the day, he had warned her about getting jealous, and really what harm was there in handing over a few meaningless facts that would set her mind at rest? "To get some fresh air. I had no intention of doing anything, if you must know. And that's that subject covered."

There were other things she would have liked to ask him—such as whether he found the mystery blonde more attractive than *her*—but she was ashamed even to think that.

"I'll have to return with my team in the morning to tidy." Her voice was still stiff as she shuffled from foot to foot, resisting the magnetic pull of his masculinity and keeping as much healthy distance as she could.

She was about to launch into the most impersonal conversation she could think of, which involved details of what rooms he wanted them to clean and whether he would provide his own cleaning service for the bedrooms once guests had vacated. She had no time. There was a rap on the door and then Beth was there, wringing her hands, clearly anxious.

Disaster: one drunk guest. All the *petits fours* on the ground, most of them crushed. The trays were all waiting to be filled, Beth practically wailed, and there was nothing much to put on them.

"Leave it to me." The diversion was a blessing in disguise because Rosie had felt her mind wandering away, gearing up for more questions about the mystery blonde, risking everything to satisfy her raging curiosity. "I have a few things in my larder. I'll work something out."

"And I'll dispatch the drunk." Angelo was walking out of the room while Beth and Rosie scurried behind him. No one batted an eye at the trio. The point about parties that were a swinging success was that inhibitions were lowered and mellow good-will prevented too many interested questions being asked about goings-on between the guests, or in this case between employer and employee. Rosie thought that her father would have adored this party and, in fairness to him, would never have fallen onto a stack of *petits fours*. Romantic melancholy had been much more his thing.

Rosie was thinking on her feet as she and Angelo dashed out to his car.

"I have boxes of biscuits and stuff on the top shelf of my larder," she was telling him as they covered the short distance between mansion and cottage. "Rainy-day stuff."

"Which is why you so richly deserved that old banger."

"You wait out here," she instructed, leaping out of the car. "I won't be a minute."

She shouldn't have been. She literally should have been five minutes, grabbing sufficient ingredients to do something clever and decorative with biscuits and dark chocolate.

Angelo waited impatiently for almost twenty minutes when, with mounting panic, he entered the cottage…

CHAPTER NINE

He found her in the sitting room where she was huddled on the sofa. She had switched on the lamp on the table next to her and it bathed her in a pool of light.

"What's going on?" Angelo came to an abrupt halt at the doorway and stared at her. Not for the first time he wondered how it was that she could draw his eyes and keep them there, as if spellbound.

Rosie looked up at him silently. She thought how events and circumstances had a weird way of altering the course of people's lives. If she had never come to London; if she hadn't been working on the one night in that bar when Angelo had happened to come; if Mandy hadn't left the cottage to her; if she hadn't reconnected in a moment of weakness after the business with Ian... The ifs could go on and on once you started listing them down.

"Well?" Angelo demanded. He flipped on the overhead light, and now he could see that she was as white as a sheet and there was a little bundle of papers in her lap with some garish costume jewellery. In one stride, he was by her, staring down at the jumble of papers. "What's all this? I've been waiting out there for you in the car. Have you forgotten that there's a party going on which we are due to return to?"

"Beth is going to take care of everything." Rosie nodded at the tins of chocolate and biscuits neatly piled on the table by the door. "All the stuff you need is right there. I've told her what to do. She's creative. She'll manage."

Angelo shook his head, confused. "I'm not paying Beth to cater my event. I'm paying *you*. So don't tell me that she can handle everything because she's *creative*." Bewilderment lent his voice a harshness that barely made Rosie flinch. She felt like a zombie, totally zoned out.

If she had known what she would find when she had begun rummaging wildly through the chaotic jumble on the top shelf of the larder, would she have begun her search for biscuits and chocolate? In her frantic haste to go as quickly as possible, she had knocked over the stack of Amanda's possessions, bits and bobs which she had shoved out of sight until the day came when she could face doing something with them—pretty tins and boxes, which she had briefly glanced at before stashing away.

And a jewellery box with a concealed drawer which had sprung open as the box had hit the tiled ground with a resounding crash, splintering open so that the gaudy baubles, stuff she'd used to wear when they had gone out as teenagers, scattered across the floor.

Rosie had the contents of the jewellery box on her lap now and she knew that, however much she didn't want to face Angelo just at this very moment in time, she had no choice.

"Angelo, we need to talk," she said heavily.

"Now is not a good time for a lengthy conversation, especially a lengthy conversation on a subject you know I have no intention of covering." He strode towards the window, then to the fireplace. For once, he wasn't grace in motion. His movements were jerky and restless and he kept glancing across at her with a frown. Instinctively he knew that, whatever was happening, it wasn't good. Instinctively, he also knew that he would rather drag things back to where they were, to the party, the biscuits and the chocolate. He could deal with her getting in a flap because she couldn't rustle up something fantastic with limited ingredients.

"We either talk, Angelo, or else you can leave and I never want to see you again. And I don't care if you don't want to cover the topics I want to cover. I don't care about your precious ground rules for this relationship."

Angelo stilled. So this was what an ultimatum sounded like; he had never had one delivered to him. He narrowed his eyes on her stricken face and got the feeling that she was close to passing out. Her breathing was fast, like someone on the verge of hyperventilating. How could all this have happened in the space of twenty minutes? Was she having some kind of panic attack?

"So talk," he said roughly. Never had he felt so at odds with himself. He wanted to continue pacing the room—he felt he needed an outlet for reserves of restless energy that he was finding difficult to contain—but then he really needed to sit, really needed to impose some calm on the situation.

"I know now," Rosie said quietly. She was glad that he had chosen not to sit next to her on the sofa but instead on one of the other chairs so that they were facing one another.

Of course she could fully see that this was the worst possible time to have this conversation, but how would she ever be able to go back up to the house with him, chat in the car as though nothing had happened, see everything through the following morning and then, when the dust from the party had settled, pull him aside for a chat? She just didn't have such reserves of self-control within her.

"What do you know?"

"A while ago I stuck some of Mandy's stuff in the larder,

right at the back on the top shelf. Actually, I'd forgotten that I'd put it there. Then, later on, I filled the shelf with bits and pieces I thought I might need one day, stuff that I could pull out in an emergency and use because the sell-by dates were way in the future..." Her voice petered out.

Angelo didn't move a muscle. He was leaning forward, head slightly cocked to one side, arms resting loosely on his thighs and his fingers lightly clasped together.

"Excellent forward-planning" was the sum total of what he could rummage up to contribute to the conversation. "You never know what you might need in a larder that has a sell-by date five years hence..."

"Beth should be here in a minute to collect all of it and take it back to your house, so you needn't worry that your friends and colleagues are going to miss out on things to eat with their liqueurs and coffee."

"This may come as a shock, but do I really strike you as the sort of man who gives a damn about something like that? Do you really think I care whether Henry from Legal has something to go with his coffee or his glass of port?"

"You paid me to do a job, so I'm going to make sure that it gets done."

"Why do I get the feeling that we're beating about the bush here?"

Rosie was saved having to answer that by the arrival of Beth who appeared in a tidal rush of concern. What did she think she had eaten? How brave of her to get through the entire evening without murmuring a word of complaint! Of course she would let everyone know that Angelo was on his way, that he was just making sure that she was okay before he headed back over...

Rosie wasn't sure what Beth suspected about her relationship with Angelo. To most people, an employer who is concerned enough to sit with his employee while she pulls herself through a bout of so-called food poisoning would be a target of instant suspicion. But Beth, aside from being incredible at what she did, was also big-hearted enough to ignore the suspicious and discreet enough to mention nothing even though suspicions had been aroused.

Certainly as she fussed and carried away the biscuits and the chocolate Rosie couldn't help but think that she and Angelo must make a very odd picture, he sitting as still as a stone, barely muttering anything; she white as a ghost and clearly distressed.

"One of Mandy's things broke. It fell and cracked open. A jewellery box." Rosie picked up the threads of the conversation as soon as Beth had slammed the front door behind her. She wanted to take this through its natural timeline—it helped, like repeating instructions out loud until they were clear in your head. A few of the brightly coloured rings and bracelets were on her lap, scooped up along with other stuff.

"When I first came across the jewellery box, I didn't even know that there was a hidden drawer under the trays of jewellery. I just opened the lid, looked in and put it aside. I know we parted company and never spoke again, but seeing her stuff brought back fond memories of how things used to be. I didn't want to get rid of the more personal pieces. I wasn't too sure what I was going to do with some of them but…" Again she faltered, twining and untwining her fingers.

Angelo had no intention of rushing her. So what if his guests began to notice his absence? He was hovering on the brink of a precipice. He could feel it, and his normally clever mind, which could cope with anything thrown at it, was not co-operating.

"But?" he eventually prompted when the silence threatened to remain permanent.

"But it's a good job I hung on to a few of her things, because how else would I ever have found out that she was having your baby?"

The silence that greeted this question was deafening. Rosie could hear her heart beating fast. So what had she been hoping for? A miracle? That he would rush into instant denial? She could tell from the greyness that stole into his face that that particular miracle was out of the question.

"What did you find?" Angelo asked eventually. Her calmness was disquieting. He thought that he would have been able to react better if she had become hysterical, argumentative, demanding. But there was a flatness behind her eyes that sent a chill through him.

"A scan picture. There was a date on it. I worked it all out." She had been confused when she had first seen it, hadn't really made any connections. When the truth had sunk in, something inside her had shrivelled up and died. She had spent years imagining that he had been having a fling with her friend, even though she just couldn't picture that in her head. Knowing the truth was even worse, because not only had they been having a fling behind her back but the fling had led to a pregnancy. Somehow that seemed like the greatest of all betrayals. He was paranoid about *them* not taking any chances, yet he had played fast and loose with Mandy. Had they sat and made plans together? Happy-family plans? Had they worked out names, projecting a future for their unborn child?

"Where is the child now? Why have you never mentioned it to me?"

Angelo was lost for words. He knew exactly what she was thinking, yet how could he confess to her that he could barely remember that one night with Amanda? How could he admit that he had been so devastated by revelations that he had practically drunk himself into a state of oblivion?

That for the first time in his life he had slept with a woman without even contributing to the act?

When Amanda had tried to insinuate herself on the back of a one-night stand he didn't remember, Angelo had turned his back on her. The fact that he had slept with her at all had disgusted him, had been a sign of staggering weakness, a moment of vulnerability of which afterwards he had been ashamed.

But when a month and a half later she had shown up with proof of a pregnancy, when it had been confirmed that the child she was carrying was his, he had been forced into a marriage he had not wanted to a woman he despised. Like it or not, his own sense of honour had become the walls of his own prison. There was no way he could allow any child of his to be born illegitimate. It just wasn't the way he was built. His mother had been great when it had come to instilling family values…not to mention the value of accepting responsibility for his actions.

"There was a miscarriage. It hadn't been a smooth pregnancy from the start. It was an early miscarriage…" Angelo could still remember that horrific day when Amanda had been rushed to hospital. Afterwards, he had asked himself whether stress had been the cause even though, when he had tentatively and privately mentioned that to the consultant he had been assured otherwise. These things happened, he had been told. It was no one's fault.

At any rate, without a child in the equation, he could easily have divorced her, but he hadn't. He had distanced himself from her, but divorce? No. His penance for being foolish enough to have been taken in by one woman and manipulated by another was to remain harnessed to Amanda for life as a reminder of his own stupidity. They had led separate lives. He had ensured her financial well-being but that was as far as it went. As far as he had been concerned, she could do as she wished, and so could he, for there was nothing binding them together. In the end, he had felt pity towards her, but that was all—and it was more than she deserved, he had always reckoned.

"I'm sorry," Rosie muttered because, whatever had happened, losing a child would have been terrible. "How long… How long had it been going on behind my back, Angelo?"

Angelo knew that this was his one and only chance to tell her the truth, but could he? At the end of the day, Rosie had been as guilty as her friend when it came to opportunism. As he was now aware, two girls from deprived backgrounds willing to do anything it took to advance their prospects. Was he now going to humiliate himself by confessing how deeply he had been affected by Rosie's betrayal? Pride surged through him, strangling at source any inappropriate temptation to confide. He wondered what he was doing here. Why had he recommenced this fatal relationship with her? All the reasons he had given himself now seemed weak and unjustifiable.

"So now you know the truth." He stood up and shrugged fluidly.

"Did you marry her because she was pregnant? Did you…did you love her?"

"I'm not discussing this."

"Is that *all* you have to say, Angelo? That you're not *discussing this?*"

"You're mistaken if you think that I'm going to indulge in some pointless heart-to-heart about it. I'm not."

"I just want to know what happened. I think you *owe* me that!"

"I don't *owe* you *anything!*"

"How can you say that?"

"We've been having sex, Rosie. Since when do I *owe*

anything to a woman I've been sleeping with? A woman who means nothing to me? Explanations are reserved for the people we care about."

Angelo steeled himself against the ugly sensation twisting inside him, as if someone had plunged a shard of glass straight through his ribcage and was methodically twisting it in search of soft tissue. This was how he had to play it. Needs must. He should never have become involved with her all over again. He should just have let sleeping dogs lie instead of thinking that he could kill off his lingering attraction to her by getting her into bed.

Rosie watched him withdraw from her, saw the ice settle over his features. She almost wished that she had never found that wretched little picture, even though the better part of her knew that it was always best to face the truth, which was something she had been dodging ever since she had jumped into bed with him. Like a fool, she was now in a position where he had had to spell things out for her: *I owe you nothing because you mean nothing to me...*

How delusional had she been ever to imagine that he would crack and open up his heart to her, give her the opportunity to defend herself? Had she ever really thought that that would happen? Or had she continued to feed her own love and addiction to him because she had secretly believed and hoped that, if they carried on with what they had, he would one day discover that he had fallen in love with her? That she had somehow become indispensable? Had she, deep down, been prepared to blank out their history if there was the promise of a future dangling in front of her? Had she imagined that he would ever be able to do the same? That somehow she could convince him to feel the same way about her as she felt about him?

"Did she take to drink because she lost the baby?" Rosie asked painfully.

"Repeat—I'm not going to discuss this." He began walking towards the door. "I have a party to get back to."

"You're just going to *go?*"

"What more ground is there to cover?"

"You're right. None." She stood up, but her legs felt wobbly. "I think we should call it a day on this. I don't want to have anything more to do with you." She was ashamed of the fleeting pause that followed this statement because she knew that, like a coward, she was giving him one last chance to jump in and somehow save the day. "I'm very sorry that I can't see the job through to the finish—but tomorrow," she said quickly, "I shall go up to the house to finish off the cleaning."

"Forget it. I'll get my people to sort it out."

"You paid me to do it."

"I said forget it."

"In that case, would you like me to return the car to you? Because that was part of the payment for ensuring that your house was returned to its pristine condition."

"Consider it a parting gift for services rendered—and I must say, you're a much cheaper option this time round."

Rosie didn't think before she raised her hand and whipped it against the side of his face. She hit him so hard that her palm stung, but it still felt good to release the rage bubbling up inside her. If she could have hit him again, she would have. She had never been prone to violence but she felt that that could change in a heartbeat, right here, right now.

Angelo rubbed the side of his face but didn't bat an eye. He supposed he deserved that.

"The next time you hear from me," he said coolly, "It'll be through my lawyer. I intend to sell my house as quickly as possible. I will suggest the necessary boundary lines, and I'll get that certified as fast as I can. Provided you don't contest my decision, it can be settled in a matter of weeks."

"Good." She was already missing him, already wondering how the weekends would be without him around. She wanted to reach out and grab him as he swung around, heading to the front door.

She didn't. Instead, she held herself in rigid silence as he strode through the door, slamming it behind him, and she remained that way until she heard the deep-throated growl of his car as it disappeared back up to his house.

Then, and only then, did she collapse, like a puppet whose strings have been cut suddenly. She sank to the ground and cried until she didn't think it was possible to have any tears left in her to shed.

In the larder, the ground was still strewn with all the stuff that had fallen off the shelf as she had scrabbled for the chocolates and biscuits. The tins and boxes, she stuffed into a bin bag. There was a coal shed at the side of the cottage; she would put it all there and maybe, just maybe, she would forget about it.

And the toxic jewellery box with its contents… It would be destined for a more permanent resting place. She put all of it in a separate bin bag and trundled the lot out to the bins at the side where they would be collected the following Monday by the bin men. In the distance, she could just about make out the sounds of revelry at Angelo's house.

It was easier not to think while she tidied and, although it was late, she cleaned the entirety of the larder, rearranging everything and wondering whether she would ever really be able to go in there without remembering the effects of tonight.

It was three in the morning by the time she finally got to sleep, after a shower. Beth had texted to ask how she was feeling and told her that the chocolate and biscuits had done the job. Rosie had read the text and had wanted to text back asking what Angelo was doing. Was he back out on the patio with the small blonde lawyer? Had he decided that sleeping with someone who didn't come with complications, baggage and a murky shared past would be blessed relief?

She still couldn't come to terms with the way he had refused to talk to her, the finality with which he had walked out of the front door without looking back. Lying in bed when she closed her eyes she still had his image in her head as he had stood in front of her and told her that he owed her nothing because she didn't matter, because he didn't care about her.

The prospect of picking up the pieces and getting on with her own life struck her as the most terrifying thing she could contemplate doing. She had tried that once and had ended up with a stalker. What was going to happen next time round? Would she land herself a serial killer?

How much poorer was her judgement going to be, because she felt as though her love for Angelo, despite all the unforgiving odds, had deepened this time round. He had been so adamant about just being in it for the sex, yet there were things they had done together that had been curiously intimate and quite unrelated to sex.

She knew that he would sell the house as fast as he could. He barely used it and he wouldn't care whether it fetched a good price or not. He didn't need the money. He would just want speed so that he could break off all connections with his past, and that included both her and Amanda.

She awoke the following morning, groggy and disoriented, and she remained in bed for an hour, letting all the memories of the night before slowly seep back into her head. When she finally began moving around, her joints felt stiff.

By mid-morning, she decided that there was only one thing to do and that was to call Jack, her confidante. He had been up to the cottage twice with his partner, mid-week when she knew that Angelo wasn't going to be around.

She could have kicked herself now for effectively putting her life on hold while she had conducted a pointless affair that had never been destined to go anywhere. She hated herself for hoping, when he had not once given her any grounds for hope, when he had repeatedly reminded her that she was just good sex and unfinished business that needed to be put to rest. Thinking back to all the conversations they'd had, she wondered how she could ever have thought that it was a brilliant idea to sleep with a man who had dumped her once, believed the worst about her, refused to hear her side of the story and had made it patently clear that he was only in it for the sex. She marvelled at the ingenuity of the human brain which could grasp incidentals—the odd kind word and tender gesture—and turn them into something meaningful. But then that was love, wasn't it? Blind to the obvious and ever willing to give the benefit of the doubt.

Jack picked up on the first ring and knew immediately that there was something wrong.

"It's Sunday," he said bluntly, cutting through the false cheer she had tried to inject in her voice. "Shouldn't you be in bed eating croissants with the Italian hunk?"

"It's over."

Rosie told him everything. She spared no details. In between her sniffling, she apologised for being a bore.

"You've been down this road before." She struggled to keep her voice even. "The last thing you need is to go down it again."

"I'm thinking the same could be said for you," Jack sympathised.

He would come the following weekend. On his own. They would have a talk and she would feel much better. Time was a great healer, he assured her with confidence, and she was ready to believe him. Maybe it was better that it ended this way because she would never now look back on the relationship with nostalgia. Anger could be a good friend when it came to forgetting things.

She was pleased for all the clichés, although they didn't make her feel any better. She was just glad that she had a friend who was willing to drop everything and travel to stay with her, where he would be obliged to listen to all her outpourings whilst insisting that he wasn't bored or tired.

Angelo stared indifferently at his mobile phone which was buzzing. He knew who it was on the other end because he had her number programmed into his address book: Eleanor French. A week ago, the day after he had slammed the door for good on his relationship with Rosie, he had made the mistake of allowing the blonde to believe that she stood a chance with him. It had been a mistake. They had been out just once and he had fought to not look at his watch, not to count the minutes, to not compare her with Rosie. The harder he had tried, the guiltier he had felt and the more he had tried to paper over his irritation by smiling. Wrong tactic. She had been calling and leaving text messages since Tuesday.

And now there was something else—the boundary lines. He had told his lawyers to draw something up and make it fast. He didn't care how much land they saw fit to sign over to Rosie. He just wanted out and he wanted to sell the house as quickly as he could.

True to their word, they had thrown the full force of their considerable combined talent into the project and the finished article was staring him in the face. On his desk. With his vibrating phone right next to it.

It was Friday. It was seven-thirty. The choice was to look over a legal document on a property he no longer wanted and certainly didn't need, which would forever cut the ties between him and a woman he likewise no longer wanted and certainly didn't need, or subject himself to another date with the piranha blonde.

He made his excuses to the blonde, this time without room for leeway or any other dates, and he began to read the legal document.

Jack's visit was good. He was cheerful and optimistic. He said all the right things and took her side without question. As he had three years before. He had shown a great deal of willingness to slag Angelo off without making any effort to see the complete picture.

In fact, *she* was the one who miserably pointed out that she only had herself to blame. She gloomily realised that she couldn't focus on all the bad things about Angelo because she was too busy thinking of all the brilliant things about him.

She discovered that it was remarkably easy to turn all his failings into endearing idiosyncrasies. He was a pig for having used her, yet hadn't she allowed herself to be used? He had never failed to remind her that there were no long-term prospects to what they had, yet couldn't you just call that honesty? He refused point-blank to indulge in anything he considered too domestic with her, yet wasn't it appealing the way he still managed to do so without even realising it? He was the most fascinating, complex and utterly infuriating man she had ever met and he was without compare.

As Jack sat in his little car on the Sunday afternoon,

revving the engine, getting ready to go, she just wanted to pull him back out through the car door and make him promise not to leave her, at least not until she was able to get her act together.

"So you've got jobs lined up?"

Rosie nodded. She couldn't have hoped for better networking opportunities than at the party Angelo had thrown. She had a list of people who were interested in commissioning her, from things as small as children's parties to an end-of-summer event to be held at the town hall.

"And we've finally finished planting up your little vegetable plot."

Yes, they had. Cultivating it would give her something to do when the nights started to draw in and winter approached.

"Plus you've joined that book club."

Something else to occupy herself now and again in the evenings.

"Not to mention volunteering to teach cookery classes at that local school."

Yep. How many more activities could one person get involved with? Jack had been great at chivvying her along, just as she had once chivvied *him* along.

"So I'll be up again on Friday. Okay?"

"You don't have to."

"I need to make sure you keep on top of those vegetables."

"You wouldn't know whether I was or wasn't, Jack."

"I can spot a weed as well as the next man."

He left with a great deal of horn-blowing and waving and Rosie retired back into the cottage.

Further up the lane, his car about to turn left into the long avenue that wound its way up to his mansion, Angelo couldn't fail to hear the blowing of the car horn. He slowed his car. The car hurtling towards him could only be coming from the cottage. Curiosity made him look at the driver of the car and he saw that face—the dirty-blond hair tied back in a pony tail, blue eyes squinting into the glare of late-afternoon sun.

A tide of rage swept over him. So the past wasn't as dead and buried as she would have liked to pretend! Had he really expected otherwise? Hadn't it always preyed somewhere at the back of his mind? Hadn't he wondered what had happened to the guy with the dirty-blond hair and the bright blue eyes?

Hell, he should never have made this trip. It had been a spur-of-the-moment decision. With the boundary lines roughly drawn up and only her consent needed to seal the deal and rid himself of her once and for all, Angelo knew that he could leave it to his lawyers to fine-tune the detail, to arrange all the necessary paperwork and documentation. But no, he had taken it upon himself to jump into his car and head down to ascertain for himself where the lines would be.

What exactly had he hoped to gain from the exercise— aside from wasting a great deal of petrol?

He certainly hadn't expected to find himself sitting behind the steering wheel of his car, consumed with such white-hot anger that he felt himself on the point of combustion.

And, even so, there was no place for his anger to go! What he *should* do, he thought grimly... No, what he was *going* to do...was to steer his car calmly up the avenue, have a last look around his house so that he could evaluate what priceless paintings and ornaments would be reshuffled to other properties he owned, have a quick tour of the land to confirm that he was in agreement with the boundary lines proposed in the deeds that were currently residing in his briefcase, and then leave. Nothing could be simpler.

He certainly would not head to the cottage and resume any sort of debate with a woman he was well rid of. A woman to whom he owed nothing. A woman who had manoeuvred him three years ago and, as was evident, had continued to manoeuvre him. A woman who schemed and lied and did it all in a way that had managed to get to him. Again!

When he looked in his rear-view mirror, it was to find that the other man's car had long since disappeared from the horizon.

Angelo swung his car away from his drive and headed towards the cottage.

He screeched to a stop in front of the cottage in a blaze of spitting gravel.

Inside, and about to begin the task of unloading the dishwasher, Rosie felt a surge of guilty relief that Jack was back, probably having forgotten something. Yet again, she was finding it difficult to be alone. The second there was no distraction, her thoughts took flight, and they always flew in the same direction.

It wasn't going to do. She knew that. She just needed her brain to start paying attention to what it surely knew it must do.

She was half-smiling as she opened the front door before the doorbell had even been rung.

More than anything else, her smile infuriated Angelo. It didn't take a genius to work out who that smile was for! In the space of the minute or so it had taken him to drive to the cottage, his mood had reached rock-bottom. Common sense had flown through the window. He seemed to have lost all sense of perspective.

"So I see old habits die hard," he gritted.

"Angelo." Rosie shrank back at the ferocious expression on his face. "What...what are you doing here?"

"You wanted to talk?" His voice was lethally cold, matching the look on his face. "Then let's do it, Rosie. Let's *talk!*"

CHAPTER TEN

"WE'VE SAID ALL there is to say to one another." Rosie found that she was shaking like a leaf and she couldn't tear her eyes away from his beautiful face. But she was determined not to be weak, not to just go along for the ride. He hadn't wanted to *talk* before. No, he had wanted to do *anything* but talk! And now here he was, looking as though he wanted to punch things, telling her that he suddenly wanted to *talk*. How was she ever going to get her life back on track if she remained vulnerable like this? If she allowed him to keep imagining that he could just show up and that she would let him in?

Besides, if he was angry over something, then she could figure out what it was. Something to do with the cottage or the land or both.

"We agreed that whatever we needed to discuss about the land would go through a lawyer." She stood in front of the doorway and folded her arms.

"I couldn't give a damn about the land. Now stand aside. I want to come in."

"And if I don't want to let you in?"

"Then—" Angelo nudged closer and she fell back "—you might find that you don't have a choice."

"How has life been treating you?" He walked past her,

his keen, green eyes searching for signs of occupation. By a man. By a man whose face was all too familiar to him.

"Fine!" Rosie stuck her chin up in mutinous response. He had headed towards the kitchen, but before she could catch up with him he was back out and making for the sitting room. From the way he glanced up the stairs, she wondered if he intended to do a full circuit of the cottage.

"I'll bet," Angelo snarled. There were no tell-tale signs of permanent occupation by someone else in the cottage, but then who knew? The bathroom upstairs might be a positive hotbed of men's razors, boxer shorts and after shave!

"What's *that* supposed to mean?"

"I should have guessed he was still around. And you had the nerve to try and wheedle personal details out of me! You're a piece of work!"

"I have no idea what you're talking about, and if you've come here to insult me then you can leave. Right away!" She wondered how she would follow that ringing command through. He was bigger, stronger and, judging from the look of it, in no hurry to go anywhere. In all the time she had known him, this barely contained savagery had never been apparent. Not for a second did she imagine that it would translate into anything physical, but she feared what he might say to her. She couldn't bear it if he began repeating how much he didn't care and had never cared about her.

Angelo laughed mirthlessly. Every time he thought about that man nonchalantly driving away from the cottage, he saw red. It was almost more than he could do just to keep up a conversation of sorts when he wanted to smash things.

"Guess what?" He walked across to the bay window and perched on the edge of it because he couldn't imagine being able to sit still.

"What?" Rosie hovered by the door, uncertain of what was expected of her.

"I saw him. So why don't we quit playing games? You can stop pretending that you don't have a clue what I'm talking about and I might finally learn the truth straight from the horse's mouth. Or should I say straight from the mouth of the scheming, lying opportunist you never stopped being?"

Rosie tentatively walked towards the sofa and sat down, drawing her legs up to her chin.

Angelo didn't take his eyes off her. God, but she was giving an Oscar-winning performance as the confused girl without an ounce of guile in her entire body. Her eyes were huge as she stared up at him. Gold-diggers usually came in sexy clothes; a few buttons undone; lashes longer than was natural; lips red and always slightly parted. She bucked the trend. Even when he had first met her in that cocktail bar, she had failed to do the part of "sexy babe" justice. Was that why he had been taken in three years ago? She was wearing her gardening garb of faded dungarees and a striped T-shirt underneath. Her feet were stuck into a pair of thick socks but she wasn't wearing any shoes.

"I honestly don't know what you're talking about, Angelo."

"Blond hair in a pony tail? Looks like a tree-hugging loser through and through? Ring any bells?"

"Are you talking about Jack?"

Angelo was enraged that she managed to maintain that steady, puzzled look even as she confessed the continuing presence of the man in her life.

"Are you going to tell me that he wasn't here? That he didn't spend the weekend in your house?" He could hear the ugly, unacceptable jealousy in his voice but he didn't care.

"Yes, he spent the weekend. What of it?"

"You disgust me."

"*I* disgust *you*?"

"Has he been on the scene all the time? I might have known that you would never have given him up!"

Rosie, about to lay into him—because how *dared* he start questioning how she lived her life?—was stunned into confused silence.

"Given him up?" she asked, bewildered.

"Spare me the butter-wouldn't-melt-in-my-mouth routine!" Angelo propelled himself away from the bay window, clenched his fists and unclenched them. "You know *exactly* what I'm talking about. You were seeing that man behind my back three years ago and you've continued seeing him behind my back this time round. What game did the pair of you have up your sleeve?"

"Seeing Jack? Yes, I've been *seeing* Jack. Why wouldn't I be? I've known him since…since *for ever*."

"You mean you aren't even going to deny your own infidelities?"

"I beg your pardon?"

"You heard me." He sat down on the chair and forced himself to keep perfectly still. It was the only way he could think of to impose some kind of self-control over emotions that were all over the place.

"You think I've been *sleeping* with *Jack*?" Rosie started laughing. She couldn't stop. She knew that there was a dangerously hysterical edge to her laughter but she just couldn't keep it in.

It was Angelo's turn to be confused. He wondered if this was a ploy. He refused to believe that he could have been wrong. No, he wasn't going to give that house-room.

"I *know* you have."

Abruptly, Rosie stopped laughing. "And you know that *how*? Because I'm just the sort of tramp who would string two men along at the same time? And was I sleeping with Jack while that creep was stalking me? And what on earth would possess you to think that Jack and I could *ever* have a relationship like that?"

"I have proof!"

"That's impossible." Rosie had the weird feeling that she had stepped into a parallel universe, one in which nothing made sense any longer.

"Pictures, Rosie. Of you. And him. Arms wrapped round one another. Laughing up at him. Him looking down at you."

Rosie heard the raw jealousy in his voice and she could see that every word he uttered was dragged out of him, as though he could no longer help himself. For the first time, she was looking at an Angelo who was *vulnerable*. Something inside her stirred and she wanted nothing more than to hold him tightly against her until that dark, devastated expression was wiped off his face.

"Where did you get those pictures from?" she asked steadily.

Angelo raked his fingers through his hair. His hands felt unsteady. "Your trusty friend showed them to me. There's no honour amongst thieves."

"Oh, Mandy," Rosie murmured.

She looked at Angelo; he glared at her and immediately said, "Don't even begin to think that you can talk your way out of this one by telling me that whatever I saw was a bunch of lies…"

"Of course Jack and I were hugging one another, and I'll bet you a million pounds I know when those pictures were taken as well." She risked standing up so that she could walk over to the comfy chair on which he was perched in tense, watchful silence.

Angelo's jaw hardened as she pulled over a small stool

to sit right alongside him. He felt like an invalid being visited by the doctor about to break bad news. He wished to God that he had never set foot inside this cottage, yet there was an inevitability to what was unfolding between them. He had laid down ground rules, had told her that the past was off-limits, but holding it at arm's length didn't mean that it ceased to exist. He hated this feeling of helplessness in the face of uncontrollable events.

"It's a long story," Rosie began. "And let's just say that Amanda took the truth and twisted it to suit her own ends."

"I'm listening," Angelo heard himself say roughly.

"The stuff I pawned…the jewellery." She took a deep breath and maintained eye contact. "I did it for Jack."

"So out comes the truth. At last." He felt as though he could do with a stiff drink, maybe more than just one. Like last time—three years ago, when he had looked at those pawn tickets and those pictures and felt like the world was closing down around him. How many more times could he be taken for a sucker?

"I wanted to tell you but I was ashamed." Rosie sighed. "You see, when the three of us decided to leave for London, well, it was a pretty bad time in Jack's life."

Angelo realised that he was thoroughly sick of hearing the man's name. He also knew that he was committed to hear the rest of what she had to say whether he liked it or not. He was finally working out what torture felt like.

"We should have left months before we did, but I didn't want to. I wanted to finish my exams. I told them I would follow but, no, we all had to go at the same time. So they waited for me and, while they waited Jack was beaten up. He almost lost his life."

"I'm not following you."

Rosie looked at him with clear eyes. "Like I said, he'd

been having a bad time, but I didn't realise just how bad until they nearly put him in hospital."

"They?" Angelo scoured her face for signs of deception but there was none. She was telling the truth, all of it.

"Gay-bashers, homophobics—call them what you want—they put him in hospital. And when he came out, and we finally made it down to London, he became drug-dependent. It was his way of coping. I…" She took a deep, steadying breath. "I blamed myself. If we'd left when we'd planned to, none of that would have happened, but I was selfish."

Angelo was lost for words. "Jack's gay?"

"I'm betting Mandy never breathed a word about that. When he finally made it out of rehab, there was a great picture-taking session. I'd bet my life that those are the pictures she showed you. Of course I had my arms around him. Of course I was laughing. I was *happy*."

"So the jewellery you pawned…"

"To help cover the cost of the best rehab place I could find. It was expensive, but he deserved it—and I know you probably think it was wrong but I don't regret a penny of it."

"Amanda."

"I'm sorry I lied to you."

"You could have said something."

"I was ashamed. I thought you'd hate me for what I'd done. It was my fault that Jack went through what he did. We broke up—well, you dumped me—and by the time I thought that I had nothing to lose by getting back in touch with you, telling you the truth, I found out that you had married Mandy." There, it was out.

"And you thought I'd been seeing her behind your back."

"She told me that you had. I just found it really hard to believe, but you dumped me. And then you went and married her, and I knew that she'd been telling the truth, and then it stopped mattering whether you knew about why I pawned the jewellery. I told myself that I was moving on. Jack was all better, had found himself a really lovely guy…"

Angelo met her eyes. Remnants of his pride rose to the surface but he knew that if he didn't tell her the truth now he would forever lose the opportunity. He reached out hesitantly to stroke her cheek and was encouraged when she didn't immediately pull back.

"I hadn't been seeing her behind your back," he said heavily. "She was just someone who shared your house. I barely even registered her. I only had eyes for you."

Rosie's breath caught in her throat and the hope she had been trying to squash, that treacherous seed of hope that had sprung into life the second she had recognised his burning jealousy, began spreading like wildfire.

"But she was having your baby."

"The night she told me about you…the man; the jewellery you'd pawned…I went out and got blind drunk because I couldn't cope." He'd thrown caution to the winds. He had laid himself bare for her to do with him as she wanted and he had experienced a weird sort of liberation. His mouth twisted. "I woke up the next morning and I was still out of it. I didn't remember her in my room, or anything else that followed."

"And she got pregnant."

"I'll never know if that was pure bad luck or whether she timed things just right. At any rate, I told her to get lost when she showed up for more of the same, but then she showed up with the news that I was going to be a father and the rest was history. I'd lost the only woman I'd ever loved and I was saddled with the one who put me in that place."

"You loved me?"

"I didn't realise how much until you were no longer around. You haunted me. I hated you for what I thought you'd done but I couldn't get you out of my mind. Amanda and I never shared a bed again. We barely shared the same space. I made sure she had more than sufficient money to do whatever she wanted, but as far as any kind of relationship went there had never been one." He pulled her gently up and Rosie sat on his lap and curved her body into his.

"You loved me," she murmured, and she felt him smile against her. "And what about now?"

"Isn't it time you committed to this conversation?" Angelo said gruffly. Even with her pressed against him he still wasn't sure that she didn't now dislike him for having made it clear that he was using her for sex.

"I love you," he inserted, already aiming to win her over if only through repetition. "I love you and I need you and I can't imagine living without you. The past week has been hell. I drove down here and I told myself that it was because I needed to personally work out where those boundary lines were going to be, but I knew that I was chancing on seeing you again. Even if all I did was argue with you. You're like a drug…"

"I like being a drug." She tilted her face up and closed her eyes as his mouth found hers and he began kissing her, a long, deep, tender kiss that left her feeling as weak as a kitten. "And, as for committing to this conversation, I've always loved you. I never stopped. I could never, ever have slept with you again if I didn't love you, although I kidded myself that I was just doing what you were doing—just dealing with unfinished business."

"I didn't divorce Amanda because I never wanted to forget my learning curve," Angelo mused. He slipped his hand under the strap of her dungarees and tugged it gently over her shoulder. "I figured I would never make the mistake of getting married again, so what was the point in getting a divorce? I was wrong. I want to get married again and this time to the only woman in the world I have ever wanted to marry. And I know I should get down on one knee and propose to you, but it's so damned comfortable having you on my lap. So, Rosie, will you be my wife?"

Rosie took a few seconds to savour the sound of that. It was something she had never, ever thought she would hear.

"I can't think of anything I'd rather be." She hooked her arm around his neck and placed a kiss on the curve of his jawbone. "You came into my life and I fell in love with you, and you're the only person I could ever imagine sharing the rest of my life with. Even when you kept telling me that it was only about the sex I still kept fantasising that one day you'd see things differently. I knew it was weak, but I just couldn't imagine you not being in my life. It was like I'd spent three years trying to forget you ever existed, and then the second I saw you again I had to live with the fact that, without you in my life, *I* didn't exist."

"And will you have my babies?" His seeking hand found the warm curve of flesh underneath her T-shirt and he smoothed his hand along her side, enjoying the way she wriggled into just the right position so that he could slip his hand under her stretchy bra and massage her breast.

"I can't think of anything I'd want more. I love you so much, Angelo. It's been a long, rough journey but I never, ever want to let you go…"

* * * * *

COMING NEXT MONTH from Harlequin Presents®
AVAILABLE AUGUST 20, 2013

#3169 CHALLENGING DANTE
A Bride for a Billionaire
Lynne Graham

Dante Leonetti is convinced Topaz Marshall is after his family's money, and he's determined to seduce the truth from her lips. After experiencing Leonetti's ferocious reputation firsthand, will she be able to resist his legendary charms?

#3170 A WHISPER OF DISGRACE
Sicily's Corretti Dynasty
Sharon Kendrick

Rosa Corretti spent one unguarded night with Kulal and now this demanding sheikh wants to control her. The more Rosa resists, the stronger Kulal's desire. But will the arrogant sheikh accept this Corretti for more than one night?

#3171 LOST TO THE DESERT WARRIOR
Sarah Morgan

Desperate to escape an arranged marriage, Layla, Princess of Tazkhan, throws herself at the mercy of Sheikh Raz Al Zahki—her family's greatest enemy! But protection has a price.... This brooding desert king is determined to make her his queen.

#3172 NEVER SAY NO TO A CAFFARELLI
Those Scandalous Caffarellis
Melanie Milburne

Poppy Silverton's home, livelihood *and* innocence are under threat from playboy billionaire Rafe Caffarelli. Poppy will fight Rafe—and her attraction to him—all the way...and be the first woman to say no to a Caffarelli!

You can find more information on upcoming Harlequin® titles, free excerpts and more at www.Harlequin.com.

#3173 HIS RING IS NOT ENOUGH
Maisey Yates

Ajax Kouros has a plan—and being jilted at the altar is *not* part of it. His company's future depends on marrying a Holt, so when his bride's sister steps up to the altar...can he say no?

#3174 CAPTIVATED BY HER INNOCENCE
Kim Lawrence

Cesare Urquart can't possibly believe any worse of Anna Henderson. But when she arrives at his sprawling Scottish estate, Cesare gets a rush of adrenaline he hasn't felt for years and soon questions every notion he's had about her....

#3175 HIS UNEXPECTED LEGACY
The Bond of Brothers
Chantelle Shaw

Sergio Castellano will do whatever it takes to keep the heir he didn't know he had. But the longer he spends with ex-lover Kristen Russell the more he realizes the cracks she once made in his armor are still there.

#3176 A REPUTATION TO UPHOLD
Victoria Parker

When wild and shameless designer Eva St. George is caught with tycoon Dante Vitale it's guaranteed to cause a headline-worthy scandal. But if they can convince the world they're truly in love they might just both get what they want....

HPCNM0813RB

*Sarah Morgan brings you her most powerful and
sensational story yet in
LOST TO THE DESERT WARRIOR*

* * *

"It was my father's dying wish that I marry Hassan."

The darkening of Sheikh Raz Al Zahki's eyes was barely
perceptible. "So why come looking for me?"

Layla had practised a hundred ways to say what she
wanted to say but every word vanished under that icy
scrutiny. "You are the rightful ruler, but if he marries me
that weakens your claim and strengthens his."

There was a sudden stillness about him that suggested
she had his full attention. "That still doesn't tell me why
you're here."

Only now did she realize just how much she'd been
hoping he'd be the one to say it. He was praised for his
intelligence, wasn't he? Couldn't he see for himself why
she was here? Couldn't he see the one solution that would
solve this once and for all?

But perhaps he could see and chose not to look.

"I don't blame you for hating us." The words tumbling
out of her mouth weren't the ones she'd rehearsed but when
she looked at him all she could think of was the loss he'd
suffered. "If I could change who I am then I would, but I'm
asking you to put that aside and do what needs to be done."

"And what," he prompted softly, "do you believe needs to be done, Princess?"

No man had ever asked her opinion. Not once, since the day she took her first step to the day she and her sister had slid out of the window of their father's bedroom. Not once had anyone treated her as anything but a weapon of the house of Al Habib.

But this man had asked her. This man was listening to her.

"You *know* what needs to be done. You have to take your rightful place. You have to end this before Hassan finishes what my father started. Before he ruins our country in the selfish pursuit of power—" She paused, wondering whether this man would be motivated more by his duty to his people than sympathy for her situation. "And to do that you have to marry me. Now. Quickly. Before Hassan finds me and takes me back."

* * *

Will Sheikh Raz Al Zahki accept this shocking proposal from Princess Layla of Tazkhan?

Find out September 2013